WHAT WE FEED
GROWS

WHAT WE FEED
GROWS

THE JOURNEY TOWARD WHOLENESS

Dr. Al L. Holloway

WHAT WE FEED GROWS
THE JOURNEY TOWARD WHOLENESS

Scripture quotations marked NIV are taken from THE HOLY BIBLE, NEW INTERNATIONAL VERSION®, NIV® Copyright © 1973, 1978, 1984, 2011 by Biblica, Inc.® Used by permission. All rights reserved worldwide.

Scripture quotations marked NKJV are taken from the New King James Version. Copyright © 1982 by Thomas Nelson, Inc. Used by permission. All rights reserved.

Scripture quotations are marked NRSV are taken from the New Revised Standard Version Bible, copyright © 1989 the Division of Christian Education of the National Council of the Churches of Christ in the United States of America. Used by permission. All rights reserved.

Scripture quotations marked RSV are taken from the Revised Standard Version of the Bible, copyright © 1946, 1952, and 1971 the Division of Christian Education of the National Council of the Churches of Christ in the United States of America. Used by permission. All rights reserved.

iUniverse books may be ordered through booksellers or by contacting:

iUniverse
1663 Liberty Drive
Bloomington, IN 47403
www.iuniverse.com
844-349-9409

Because of the dynamic nature of the Internet, any web addresses or links contained in this book may have changed since publication and may no longer be valid. The views expressed in this work are solely those of the author and do not necessarily reflect the views of the publisher, and the publisher hereby disclaims any responsibility for them.

Any people depicted in stock imagery provided by Getty Images are models, and such images are being used for illustrative purposes only. Certain stock imagery © Getty Images.

ISBN: 978-1-6632-2581-8 (sc)
ISBN: 978-1-6632-2579-5 (e)

Library of Congress Control Number: 2021913830

Print information available on the last page.

iUniverse rev. date: 07/13/2021

CONTENTS

ACKNOWLEDGMENT

God bestows the gift of physical life for all of those conceived and has drawn even a momentary breath of life. The social construct of time may mean something for you and me but it lacks relevancy for an Infinite God. The gift remains a gift, no matter how brief the physical existence. Within the gift of physical life, God grants us the uniqueness of a person as distinct as our fingerprints. God has gifted me with an inquisitive and analytical mind with a desire to write. As a servant of God, with the desire to write, I wish to serve God well with my writings, and with every book, I tribute to God its accomplishment. If my words help to draw the reader closer to God, I am honored and I praise God for His gift, guidance, and inspiration. Whatever errors or misconceptions are written in this book is totally mine to own.

In addition, there have been tremendous historical and contemporary exemplars that brilliantly illuminate the way for spiritual seekers. Their physical presence in this material world has greatly touched thousands upon thousands of people. However, what I have been equally impressed by is the enumerable, yet unassuming spiritual exemplars that are touching lives in subtle ways. They have entered into the pure-heart realm with humility, perhaps appearing to blend into the background. They are service-oriented, gentle in spirit, generous in heart, and loving in action. During the course of writing this book, I have been inspired by two such exemplars: Ms. Julie Peterson (WMHC) and Ms. Faye Wooten (MPS). Both are unobtrusive and would likely deny that they are worthy of this recognition; which, is ultimately a testament that they do.

PROLOGUE

Bishop T.D. Jakes, dubbed "America's Pastor," is the pastor of a nondenominational church in Dallas, Texas (The Potter's House). During one of his televised sermons, he made a statement about feeding that which feeds you. I took that to mean that we all have a mutual responsibility to invest in the things that we are extracting dividends from. I surmised that he was talking about his ministry and it certainly makes sense for all television ministries to promote this. After all, they can't continue to "feed" us spiritually on a grand scale if we are not "feeding" the ministry monetarily. T.D. Jakes, Joel Osteen, and Joyce Meyers appear to be genuine and authentic servants of God, with sermons that resonate within my soul (though I am not oblivious to the social media criticism that even they have received).

I don't want to herald the critical voices that always find fault in what people do, but I also don't want to dismiss them either. It may be hard to fathom the value of spiritual pursuits when Ms. Joyce Meyers is "Enjoying Everyday Life" with an estimated net worth of eight million dollars, and Bishop Jakes will preach from the Potter's House but doesn't live in a "pauper's house" with his estimated net worth of 20 million dollars, and Pastor Joel Osteen's soft-spoken mannerism is raking in an estimated net worth of 100 million dollars. Therefore, each truth-seeker must exercise spiritual discernment to determine what is palatable for their spiritual digestion. Christ, Himself, was mocked, criticized, and condemned, so with all fallible people (including myself), when the seeker of truth bites into the fruit of the spirit that we are handing out, make sure that there is nothing rotten in what you are consuming. I, as a therapist, continue to align our capacity for greater mental health with the essence of our spiritual development. If this is palatable to your tastes, take another bite. If not, spit it out (as this book will have nothing to offer you).

Not unlike the truth of Bishop Jakes' assertions that we are to feed the things that feed us, I recognize that many of us who struggle with mental health (not all) are failing to adequately feed our spirit and our mental capacity is withering on the vine; hence the title for this book, "What We Feed Grows." We are on a developmental journey for greater spiritual awareness and comportment. Christ is the Light in a world of darkness; the Way on our journey back home to God; and the Bread that nourishes our spiritual life. As affirmed by the Disciple John, "... *Jesus said to them, 'I am the bread of life. He who comes to Me shall never hunger, and he who believes in Me, shall never thirst'*" (John 6:35, NKJV). I don't begrudge anyone of his or her wealth and nor am I envious of it, but the incessant pursuit of mammon diverts our paths from God.

If this sound more like Christian proselytizing and less about the psychology of mental health, forgive me, as I am not trying to promote religion here; rather, I am promoting greater spiritual awareness and good mental health. When we satiate our hunger on the legitimate spiritual ideals that are represented by Christ we cease having an appetite for the illegitimate hunger needs (wants) that keeps us trapped in ignorance with addiction to the material world. The Light of Christ-Consciousness illuminates our path that facilitates greater mental health. God is not the architect for a disturbed mind, and Christ (along with all spiritual exemplars) illuminates a pathway for peace. Each of us has an important journey upon this earthly plane with free agency to choose. We choose the things that we will ingest, and the things that we feed on give us vitality or generate our despair.

"What we feed grows." Whether it is a television ministry, a backyard garden, or the fruit of the spirit (that is associated with greater mental health) we must sow into it to produce the harvest that we are to receive. Bishop Jakes, Joyce Meyers, Joel Osteen are present-day spiritual exemplars feeding the souls of Americans and beyond. Others are destined to thwart our spiritual progression; whether charlatans who are purposefully exploiting us or those residing in darkness simply valuing our company.

The blind (spiritually uninitiated) are not good path-pointers. Those with an authentic, sincere, relationship with God are obliged to illuminate the path for others to see. I choose to follow any spiritual exemplar that righteously leads the way and will lead those by example who choose to follow. Nevertheless, at the end of the day, we are called to, *"Trust in the Lord with all your heart and lean not on your own understanding; in all your ways acknowledge Him, and He shall direct your paths"* (Proverbs 3:5-6, NKJV).

INTRODUCTION

Monotheism is the hallmark of "Western" religions of Judaism, Christianity, and Islam. Perhaps "Abrahamic" religions are a more appropriate descriptor, as none of the three monotheistic religions originated in the West. On the other hand, Eastern religions tend to be more Asiatic in origin (i.e., China, India, Japan, etc.) and represent a wide variety of religious orientations (e.g., polytheism, non-theism, animism, etc.). Christianity is perhaps a hybrid of monotheism in the sense that there is a singular God; but also, a Triune God (i.e., Heavenly Father, Divine Son, and Holy Spirit). Nevertheless, within the 6-10 thousand years of human history (perhaps hundreds of thousands or millions of years from an evolutionary perspective), Abraham's relationship with The One God substantially changed people's religious beliefs and spiritual pursuits.

I value the Christian perspective (without disavowing any other viewpoint) because this triune perspective best serves my orientation to life. That is, from a spiritual perspective, God the Father represents the Creator and Sustainer of the entire universe. The Son represents the Exemplar for our daily living. Simultaneously, The Holy Spirit represents the Connector of Animate and Inanimate Objects. The Three Distinct Entities are The One and The One is represented by Three Distinct Entities. This trinity is useful when I consider our very makeup of being spiritual, mental, and physical beings. This trinity is reflected within our spiritual journey to wholeness (i.e., indifferent-heart, craving-heart, and pure-heart realms). Lastly, this trinity aligns well with my profession as a psychotherapist edified by three basic schools of thought (i.e. psychoanalytic, cognitive, and behavioral).

"Integrity" per Stephen Carter in his similarly entitled book, identifies three interlocking concepts relating to integrity as discerning one's truth, speaking one's truth, and comporting one's behaviors to what one thinks and asserts as being true. Integrity, or the integration of oneself, is what I strive for within this healing profession. Integrity is pulling together our disparate pieces (both good and bad) into a concentrated whole with acceptance and love of the totality of who we are. Indeed, it is the lack of integrity that creates a fragmented ego state; thereby, much of our mental disorders. Of course, there are organic mental illnesses that have an unrelenting grasp upon some people. Schizophrenia, fetal alcohol syndrome, dementia, and the like trap people within an inescapable physiological/neurological condition that impairs cognitive functioning, leisure or occupational functioning, and interpersonal relationship functioning. However, a "functional" (vs. organic") mental health disorder (which ought to be labeled "dysfunctional" due to the impairment in functioning) allows for talk therapy and spiritual transformation (the renewal of our minds) to have some resonance.

The Diagnostic Statistical Manual of Mental Disorders (5th edition), provide guidance for clinicians to "accurately" diagnose one's mental condition. "Crazy, insane, or possessed" are pejorative labels that do nothing to assist people struggling with mental disorders. As stated above, three areas of impairment that denote a mental illness are related to leisure, interpersonal connections, and vocational stability. This stems from the three overarching mental maladies of anxiety, depression, and psychoticism. Of course, there are biological (genetic), interpersonal (familial or social networks) and social factors (political, geographical, social-economic status, etc.) that contribute to our mental wellbeing (or lack thereof), but I would argue that much of our mental distress stems from a misalignment within our triune self of spiritual, mental, and physical essence. I've equated the three aspects of our human essence in my previous book (The Ugli Fruit) to a corporation or agency. That is, the board of directors (spirit) determines the vision and mission of the organization. The board brings upon a CEO (mind) to develop a strategic plan and bring on the necessary staff to fulfill the vision/mission established by the board and lastly the "worker bees" or the staff (physical) is essential for fulfilling the vision/mission, goals/objectives, and service/production of the organization.

Likewise, as spiritual beings having a human experience, our level of spiritual differentiation will create our vision and inform our mission. If our spirit is impaired, our mind constructs a strategic plan to fulfill the distortions of an impaired spirit and the body will carry out the defective plans conjured up in our mind under the auspices of spirit. Nevertheless, whether it is religion (Christianity), the essence of who we are (spirit), the organization of where we work, the psychological school of thought, or our psychological wellbeing, each is orchestrated around a trinity. Our spiritual journey is no exception, in that we are on the pathway from the deep-seated ignorance residing within the indifferent-heart realm to the intellectualizing or rationalizing in the craving-heart realm to the equanimity that flows from an enlightened view within the pure-heart realm.

This book, "What We Feed Grows," reminds us that we are on a spiritual pathway and the effort made to reintegrate our individual selves advance us toward reunification with God. With thousands of psychometric tests and screenings, numerous theoretical psychological orientations, and treatment approaches, many of these either efficacious or confounding approaches can be reduced down to the simplicity of spirituality. I expressed to clients that therapy is not that complicated. I have previously written on my whiteboard that "There is no magic in therapy. It is hard work," but the essence of therapy is simple. I explain to my clients that there are three parts to my therapeutic approach when utilizing a Solution-focused therapeutic approach. I inform clients that we must accurately deduce what the problem is, we must take ownership of our role in creating or maintaining the problem, and lastly, we must be willing to change the trajectory of what produced the problem. In effect, therapy is as simple as "name it, claim it, and change it."

If I can break through the clients' defenses and impart within them that we are each upon a spiritual journey toward wholeness (ego integrity) and then they can be aware of their personal responsibility to take action in line with the direction they choose to go. "Direction" is a part of our spiritual essence (i.e., meaning, purpose, direction and connection) but no therapist can compel a client to go in a direction that the client refuses to go ("there is no magic in therapy"). Many come, perhaps for the amelioration of their distressing symptoms, but few are willing to change their lives. The adulteress doesn't want to end her affair but seeks therapy because her paramour constantly lies to her and she feels hurt by his deceit, with little attention paid to her own deceit. The client struggling with alcohol wants to appease his girlfriend by attending therapy while denying that he is still drinking. The woman with broken ribs rationalizes the assault as a testament to how much her partner really loves her, with no intention of extricating herself from her egregious abuser. Healing cannot be achieved when clients fight with therapists to remain stuck.

God, in His infinite wisdom and abiding love has granted us a gift of life for spiritual beings to have a physical experience with personal agency and autonomy. We are empowered to choose the direction of our journey and what we will ingest to facilitate our journeys. We understand the notion that "we are what we eat." Likewise, "whatever we feed will grow." If we feed our self-interests with hedonism, this will grow. If we feed our spirit with spiritual attributes, this will grow. If we feed on joy, love, kindness, etc., it diminishes the prospect of depression, anxiety, and derision of others. I, as a spiritual sojourner and mental health professional, want people to have greater mental stability. I want people to have greater interpersonal connectivity. I want people to choose professions that feed their souls. I want people to recognize that their journey toward wholeness is aligned with the attributes of the Most High God. I want a lot for your healing and fulfillment of your spiritual journey but each journey (even within the company of others) is a solitary journey and the destination is contingent upon what you want and what you choose to feed.

THE JOURNEY TOWARD WHOLENESS

Show me Your ways, O LORD;
Teach me Your paths.
Lead me in Your truth and teach me,
For You are the God of my salvation;
On You I wait all the day.
(Psalm 25: 4-5, NKJV)

In the first chapter of Moses' fifth book in the Bible, Deuteronomy, Moses (the emancipator of the Israeli people from the unrelenting grip of the Egyptian Pharaoh Ramses) discusses an eleven-day journey taking over 40 years to make. Israel's 430 years of enslavement was originated by the goodwill bestowed upon Joseph by the Egyptians, whose God-gifted ability to interpret dreams, literally saved all of Egypt and Israel from a devastating famine. Over the course of time, with new Egyptian authorities that ruled who had no allegiance to Joseph, favor shifted to fear, and fear resulted in Israel's enslavement. Those chosen for greatness are suddenly thrown into indentured servitude, suffering from all the indignities that stem from segregation and subjugation. The psyche and/or spirit of any people enduring generations of slavery can cause irrevocable damage.

During this subjugation endured by the people of Israel, the enslaved cried out for years that God intercede in their plight. Generations of "God's chosen people" suffered despicable and inhumane indignities, incomprehensible abuse, and inescapable death. Children were born into a world having never tasted freedom. Slaves were underfed; thus, malnourished but still conscripted in servitude from daybreak until dusk. Illnesses and injuries were ignored. Weeping was met with indifference. Women were violated by their overseers. Beatings became the order of the day and whether one died or was killed they were unceremoniously disposed of with less care than we in the 21st Century grant our recyclable trash.

God heard the people's cry and though God's response may have seemed inordinately protracted for those in the midst of suffering but the passing of time, adversity, and the aforementioned suffering shapes people into instruments that can be used in the service of God. As directed by God, and under the stewardship of Moses, the Israeli people marched out of Egypt with gold, silver, jewelry, flocks of fowl, and herds of animals. Indeed, within a moment, the captive Israelis went from being impoverished to wealthy, enslavement to emancipation and from despair to elation. The physically weak, fragile, and infirmed, supported by their kinsmen were overjoyed in witnessing the salvation of the Lord. God had done what was promised and rescued these people from further generations of cruelty.

Whether we are examining the beginnings of human origins with Adam and Eve or examining the psyche of humanity in the 21st Century our memory, gratitude, and appreciation is often short-lived. That is, despite the tremendous miracles demonstrating God's grace, guidance, and love, the fractured, yet freed Israelis bickered, complained, and vocalized their desire to go back to the misery they were familiar with versus trusting God (or Moses) to direct their path. Traumatized people struggle in reaching the fullness of their being. Trauma erodes one's sense of safety and security. The effect of trauma is like pricking a tire and one's spiritual essence seeps outside of him or her. Traumatized people struggle in forging a healthy relationship with God. They often feel betrayed, abandoned, or deny the existence of God. They are governed by the effects of the trauma that may cause them to engage in self-harming behaviors, promiscuity, risky pursuits, anger outbursts, learned helplessness, codependency on their abusers, indulgence in mind-altering intoxicants, and other self-destructive behaviors. Our ego integrity or spiritual development that is impacted by trauma can disrupt our path to salvation but our pathway is also obscured by the degree of our spiritual development.

During our infancy we are obtuse. Why wouldn't we be? There is no frame of reference shaped by lived experiences or shared accounts from others that we can attest to during our infancy. Mirroring is occurring but no one would expect an infant to have the wherewithal of an adult. We enter into an experience, no matter what it is, with an absence of experiential knowledge. When we are born we have no concept of how to navigate the physical world and our survival is totally contingent upon the goodwill of care providers. During our infancy we suck off of teats for nourishment and gradually start to consume pabulum but this is all we can appropriately digest at this stage of development. There is nothing defective or flawed about our inability to consume more substantial meals because in this early stage of development this is all we can handle.

Likewise, during our spiritual development, we each start off in our infancy. We are oblivious to spiritual matters or ideals; indeed, we really don't care about these matters. After all, what infant cares one iota about the karmic law that we reap what we sow? We consume what is put before us, trusting that those who have lived lives before us will nourish us adequately in order for us to advance to our next developmental level. Of course, we are uniquely different and some mothers will breastfeed (or bottle feed) a child until he or she is 2-3, 5-6 or 12-13 years old! I know of adults suckling from a bottle in their 20's and 30's. Whether this behavior is a compulsion or fad, one would think that the sting of social stigma would damper anyone's enthusiasm for nursing on a bottle in their 30's but some are very proud of this behavior and promote it to others.

Religiously (or spiritually) speaking these people have arcane or unchanging fundamental beliefs about their spiritual ideas. Not unlike the "chosen people" of Abraham being exposed to monotheism in a bifurcated world, people continued to set up camps of division with a narrow understanding of right and wrong; along with adhering to religious dogmatism versus spirituality. They feasted upon what they've heard; perhaps spitting some of it up, but their "religious mothers" may scrape this spat-up food off the babies chin and feed it right back to them. The consumers and feeders of this "pabulum" are not bad people. They give and receive to the extent of their knowledge with an unwillingness to consume anything else or grow beyond their developmental level. They are as lost as the Israelis were in fleeing a trauma-filled past into an uncertain future (*"Show me Your ways O Lord…"*).

This religious or spiritual infancy I have equated in former writings as the indifferent-heart realm. Those operating within that indifferent-heart realm have spiritual ignorance so profound, that no one can or will be able to budge them from their fundamental views. God didn't bother to convince the uninitiated members of Abram's family that He was/is an Absolute, Sovereign, and Singular God. Rather, God took the initiated Abram (the one that was in a relationship with Him) and directed Abraham away from the contagious influences of those remaining in darkness. I admire this stance being replicated in the New Testament with Christ's patience and restraint in not trying to convince the spiritually uninitiated of spiritual ideas. *"He who has ears to hear, let him hear!"* (Matthew 11:15, NKJV). This is also sound advice for therapists who try in vain to reshape the core beliefs of those residing in the indifferent-heart realm.

I squirm a bit when I reference some people's spiritual development as "infantile, childish or ignorant." I recognize that my own ignorance is profound. I constantly remind people that even with a doctorate degree, I couldn't fill a thimble with the knowledge that I have acquired about the mysteries of this universe. God is not calling upon us to understand the vast mysteries of the universe but to focus upon our own spiritual development. Nevertheless, I can see this profound ignorance and intransigence in the clients I have attempted to serve who argue for their right to remain with an abusive partner, to continue having relationship trysts, or to continue indulging within the illegal substances that are ruining their lives. It is through this understanding that I created the spiritual differentiation scale that I have introduced to readers in my book, "The Fruit of the Spirit: A Primer for Spiritual Minded Social Workers."

Within the bulk of my therapy sessions, I introduce the continuum of our spiritual journey on the whiteboard with the illustration I have placed in this book to help provide greater clarity about our journey to wholeness (see Journey to Wholeness illustration). Of course, this "wholeness," "self-actualization," or "fully integrated ego-state" are merely synonymous concepts that I've associated with the "pure-heart realm." A spiritual awakening not only happens within the pure-heart realm, but it is also exemplified in our behaviors. The journey of reclaiming self and the ultimate fellowship with God is encapsulated in the above scripture, "*Show me Your ways O Lord; Teach me Your paths…*" It is within each of these realms that our paths will be pursued and who we are is revealed. The indifferent-heart realm is represented as a deflated or fragmented ego-state. We are self-focused with a distorted view of ourselves; thus, behaving reactively. When our spiritual resources are depleted, resulting from a fragmented sense of self, we still have legitimate hunger needs (e.g. love, respect, validation, appreciation, etc.) but due to our ignorance, we fill the empty spaces within us with illegitimate desires (e.g., drugs, alcohol, porn, anger, doubt, etc.). The fragmentation of self is caused by spiritual, mental, emotional, or physical insults; which, in turn, are the trauma wounds causing "hurting people to hurt others" (or hurt ourselves) and "broken people to break things."

When we lack a secure foundation of which we are, we operate out of fear. There are literally hundreds of references relating to fear in the Bible. We are instructed to "fear not." Fear creates a reactive response where we avoid the thing that we fear or we attack and destroy the thing that we fear. Additionally, fear can create a frozen response with immobilization and intransigence. On May 25, 2020, the world woke up to the plight of black people and our interactions with police officers producing a deadly outcome that was captured on video. The world watched the handcuffed and prone, George Perry Floyd, Jr. (a black man) having his life snuffed out of him by Derrek Chauvin (a white man). Chauvin, a Minneapolis police officer at the time, pressed his knee on the neck of Floyd for eight minutes and forty-six seconds, despite the pleas of Floyd that he couldn't breathe and the pleas from onlookers that Chauvin was killing Floyd.

Journey to Wholeness

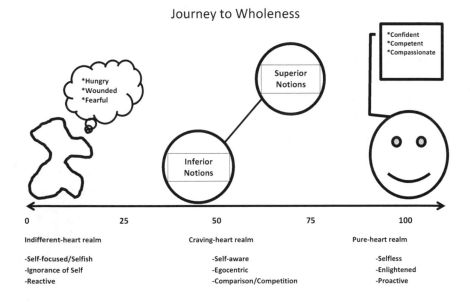

Indifferent-heart realm

-Self-focused/Selfish
-Ignorance of Self
-Reactive

Craving-heart realm

-Self-aware
-Egocentric
-Comparison/Competition

Pure-heart realm

-Selfless
-Enlightened
-Proactive

The murder of Floyd was despicable and unconscionable! It depicted the long-ignored cries of minorities at the hands of majority people stemming from the European co-optation of this country from indigenous people. Floyd was not a "saint" (nor is the vast majority of all people) and Chauvin is not a "monster." To make Chauvin into a monster separates him out from who we are (and I'm fully aware that "there but for the grace of God go I"). I certainly don't want to minimize the apparent racism that was exhibited for the world to see but was there something other than racism that held Floyd on the ground by the knee of Chauvin? Biological brothers, Cain killed Abel; Fellow Jews killed Christ; Fellow Hindus killed Gandhi and fellow Muslims killed Malcolm X (El-Hajj Malik El-Shabazz). Race was not a factor in these historical murders and lest you think that gender and child status is a protective factor from human cruelty, I want to remind you of the attempted assassination of the youngest Nobel Prize winner, Malala Yousafzai (shot three times by the Taliban for merely advocating for the right of females to be educated).

I wish I can give credit to the white male speaker I heard on the radio approximately 15 years ago regarding race relations in America, but he made a statement that I have never forgotten. He expressed that white people (his people) have a "rabid fear of black empowerment." Wow! That was a striking and stunning admission by this Caucasian brother and advocate for improving race relations. Likewise, Internal Family Systems (IFS) creator, Richard Swartz wrote, "When the source of bigoted thoughts is ignorance or socialization, then challenging and overriding them makes sense, and providing information and experiences that counter them is very useful. But, like many other cognitive-based interventions, education alone may not touch the emotionally charged parts that are embedded in our limbic systems." The limbic system is where base emotions reside, like pleasure or fear and the ingrained fear of the other is endemic to all people. A problem must be accurately named if a solution is to be found and the notion that whites have a "rabid fear of black empowerment" was eye-opening for me. It was a statement that jarred me because it is fundamentally true and a white person had the courage to say this.

Here again, I want to be careful not to dilute the arguments about race but fear is not relegated to race. Fear is not an attribute of God; thus, our journey to wholeness moves us away from fear. Christ's disciple John reminds us that God is Love; therefore, *"[t]here is no fear in love; but perfect love casts out fear, because fear involves torment"* (I John 4:18, NKJV). Ego (that which sees itself as separate and distinct from others) is the antithesis of what God is and the progenitor of fear. Ego indulges in a bifurcated world of extremes or opposites. Martin Luther King, Jr., in his book, "Strength to Love," wrote, "… [T]he history of man is the story of the struggle between good and evil. All of the great religions have recognized a tension at the very core of the universe." In order for ego to separate and distinguish itself from the other, it must create an "other dynamic" for this to happen. There are rich and poor, male and female, white and black. When separation occurs, based upon these distinctions, we tend to evaluate these distinctions by making upward and downward comparisons. That is, rich is considered better than poor; male trumps being female and white is preferable to black. With that faulty measuring stick in place, it is no wonder why we have strife amongst the people.

The concept of fear has its own bifurcated extremes of avoidance or attack. My fear of snakes would cause me to avoid them at all cost; however, if one slithered into my home, I may go into a manic attack mode trying to destroy the snake with any object at my disposal. Fear blocks our capacity for understanding, empathy, or compassion. Chauvin (white) sees his superiority in being human; thereby, contrasting himself with Floyd (black) that he perceives as inhuman. He operates out of fear by avoiding who he perceives as inhuman (Floyd) with lack of understanding, empathy, or compassion and then engaged within an attack. I can see Cain's "rabid fear" of Abel's empowerment (or favor) by God. Jews felt "rabid fear" when their authority was challenged by this young upstart guy calling himself the "Son of God." "Rabid fear" raised its ugly head when fellow Hindus felt that Gandhi was allowing the partitioning of India into two separate nation-states (India and Pakistan). Malcolm X stepped away from the Nation of Islam; which was akin to a jealous spouse fearing abandonment by his or her partner and prompting his assassination. And, Yousafzai's attempted murder was a result of female empowerment scaring the "bejesus" out of Taliban men who are used to male superiority and the oppression of women.

Our spiritual development shifts again when we enter the craving-heart realm. The ego is not as fragmented or distorted as it is in the indifferent-heart realm. The patently pervasive ignorance operating in the indifferent-heart realm gives way to the ego's awareness of self in the craving-heart realm. There is a distinctive hierarchical difference where we see ourselves in comparison with, the contrast in, and competition between other ego-states. This dynamic doesn't appear to be as cruel as what might exist in the indifferent-heart realm (though nuanced and subtle bigotry can be as insidious as overt bigotry); nevertheless, this hierarchical separation creates conflict, distance, and cutoffs. Within this realm, we may see more micro-insults or micro-aggressions. That is, the visceral hatred that may occur between races within the indifferent-heart realm gives way to benign separation endemic of white privilege within the craving-heart realm.

The path of the craving-heart has humanistic and ego-centric appeal. This is a performance-oriented realm where differences can generate affluence, status, and prestige. Political and religious elites set up social structures (governments, churches, penal and educational systems, etc.) along with social forces (culture, social media, racism, sexism, etc.) to solidify their power and to control the masses. Male patriarchy, stemming from the very first man, Adam, sets up male/female divisions with men at the top and this dynamic is reemphasized with Apostle Paul's epistle to the Ephesians, *"Wives, submit to your husbands, as to the Lord. For the husband is head of the wife…"* (Ephesians, 5:22-23; NKJV). Perhaps the Apostle Paul, formerly the persecutor of Christians known as Saul, would not have condoned wives submission in the manner that this subjugation of women has been seen throughout the years but I suspect many women would like to have seen Paul write, "Husbands, submit to your wives…"

The pure-heart realm is based upon egalitarian relationships. There is knowing and competency in this realm, *"Be still and know that I am God…"* (Psalms 46:10, NKJV). There is knowing and confidence in this realm, *"Fear not, I am with you; Be not dismayed, for I am your God"*

(Isaiah, 41:10, NKJV). There is knowing and humility in this realm, *"Humble yourselves in the sight of the Lord and He will lift you up"* (James, 4:10, NKJV). There is knowing and action in this realm, *"whatever you want men to do to you, do also to them,"* (Mathew 7:12, NKJV). Christ is a preeminent exemplar operating in this realm as a servant-leader. He is the "way, truth and life" that we emulate in the pure-heart realm. Christ responded to Peter when Peter expressed opposition to Christ washing his feet, *"If I then, Your Lord, have washed your feet, you also ought to wash one another's feet. For I have given you an example, that you should do as I have done to you"* (John, 13:14-15; NKJV).

The pure-heart realm is not demanding perfection from any of us. After all, we are all imperfect beings doing our best to navigate the world at whatever developmental level that we are at, but it does require discernment and having our heart turned toward the Ultimate with our imperfect trek toward wholeness. We are men and women striving to become people of integrity so that we, too, can be exemplars for others. Selfless beings are not naïve or gullible. We are not patsies or chumps but are individuals that have committed to a path based upon our discernment of truth that is exemplified within our lives. The concept of "enlightenment" within the pure-heart realm is merely having knowledge of our true selves plus action steps. Per Maya Angelou, "Do the best you can do until you know better. Then when you know better do better."

"Show me Your Ways O Lord; teach me Your paths…" is the sentiment echoed in the hearts of those operating within the pure-heart realm. It is the path that transcends ignorance and hedonism. It supersedes competitiveness and comparisons. It is Christ's example of not only knowing but also serving as a way of life. It is only within the pure-heart realm where the "fruit of the spirit" ripens, is harvested, dispensed, and consumed. Those in the indifferent-heart realm do not sow seeds for fruit production. Those within the craving-heart realm cogitate, intellectualize and debate about the seeds to be planted. Whereas, those within the pure-heart realm have certitude about the seeds to be planted, as those seeds are the attributes of God, and they readily cast these seeds with hopes of bountiful productions. This bounty (in the pure-heart realm) is not hoarded for self-indulgence

within storage bins or silos, nor is it produced to one-up ourselves over others, but to generously be dispensed to those in need.

The essence of spirit (i.e. meaning, purpose, direction, and connection), I've articulated well within my book, "The Ugli Fruit: Tapping the Inner Spirit for Greater Mental Health." "Direction" implies knowing the place where we resided on the spiritual continuum and where we are heading on that continuum. The darkness of ignorance in the indifferent-heart realm greatly distorts our vision, with an incessant grasping of the material world and hearts turned away from God. There is an innate spiritual desire to reclaim our full spiritual selves; thereby, returning to the Ultimate Essence of God but the awareness of this journey is contingent upon our level of spiritual differentiation. It is only when we arrive at the craving-heart realm or pure-heart realm that we can contemplate and act on the "*ways of God*" or the "*paths of God.*"

One's religious and/or spiritual awareness and practice reveal our placement on the pathway to God. "I'm not religious," boast some people. "I am religious," boast some others. There is value in our religious and spiritual development, thus, it is important to be aware of, edified by, and practice within each. The church is a collective. It is the multiple branches that shoot off from the vine. The church...denomination...religion is designed for edification and support for spiritual development. A great boon for United States preeminence on the world stage in the 19th Century was the nation's investment in free public primary and secondary education. This education is not only free to the consumer but compulsory because political leaders, corporate CEO's and academics were prescient enough to realize that the nation was transitioning from an agricultural-based economy to the industrial-based economy, and an educated workforce was paramount.

Likewise, the church pools people together for a common purpose of edification and instruction in religious matters to enhance our spiritual capacities, to facilitate our spiritual growth. A relationship with God is not just prayer but an ongoing study to know the Essence of God. Our knowledge of God changes from rudimentary and literal interpretations to critical analysis and metaphorical understandings to a transcendent relationship with God. Our religious connections and study shape our morality. We have an intuitive sense about what's right and wrong but our morality also needs to be nurtured and developed. We are naturally drawn to hedonism but our morality redirects our steps toward God. Of course, stiff, rigid and punitive morality can push us away from God but developmentally our external locus of control is needed to develop an internal locus of control. The tenets, rituals, and structure of religion provide a foundation or fertile ground when planting seeds for our spiritual development.

The absence of a religious foundation and spiritual development is not necessarily devoid of goodness. I don't know this to be true, but I can imagine that some of the great pioneers in discovering a vaccine for this terrible coronavirus (COVID-19) are avowed atheists. Nevertheless, their position would be lower on the spiritual continuum because an atheist view is the antithesis of a faith-based God. The opposite of life is death and the opposite in recognition of the Goodness of God is evil. To be clear, evil beings can exhibit behaviors that we all attest are "good" (i.e., grabbing the door for you as you enter a building or fund a scholarship that gets you through school) but the person's heart is turned away from God. Evil is the word "live" spelled backward and to sin is to live our lives backward by turning our backs on God. Atheists, who are non-religious and non-spiritual (NR/NS), boldly declare their denial of the Source that brings forth their very life.

Of course, we can have people indoctrinated within religious dogma (not doctrine, as they probably don't know their religious holy book), who are not spiritual and can inflict cruelty upon others. Religious and non-spiritual people (R/NS) have a religious structure with unorthodox rules and unquestioning devotion to a leader who purports to have special status and/or a relationship with a deity. Often these are charismatic, grandiose, narcissistic, and antisocial men preying on the naivety and vulnerability of others. Branch Davidians were represented by David Koresh, the People's Temple was led by Jim Jones, and NXIVM cult, as founded by Keith Raniere are all examples of a collective of religiously

12

indoctrinated people who lack a vision of spirituality. God is an Expansive Being and these are narrowly contrived religious cults excluding others and exploiting its membership. Lest you think that narrow religious indoctrination occurs only within fringe religious groups, members of the KKK, adopting Christian religion fall with this classification of having a religious orientation and lacking spirituality.

Those with a broad spiritual orientation and an eclectic religious underpinning, which are spiritual and non-religious (S/NR), are certainly more advanced on the spiritual continuum than the preceding groups but lack a structured religious foundation. Some might say, "That's great!" Unfortunately, some people feel an oppressive yoke of institutionalized religions stymieing their spiritual development, but if everything goes then nothing stands, so there must be some fundamental truism that lays a foundation for spiritual growth. The Church, whether institutionally based or congregate based serves an important function. Likeminded people come together as study buddies and for support as they strive to understand the incomprehensible (God). Fallible people produce fallible institutions but the value of religious indoctrination, tradition, and rituals is designed to formerly inculcate spiritual sojourners on their path toward wholeness.

Though imperfect, religions…religious institutions…churches provide an important foundation for introducing, developing, and honing our spiritual essence. My spiritual development was greatly aided by the readings of many religious texts (i.e., Bible, Bhagavad Gita, Dhammapada, Quran, Vedas, etc.). They are wonderfully rich documents of historical accounts, poetry and prose, allegories, inspirational narratives, motivational proverbs, moral instruction and guidance for conduct, cognitive reframes (renewal of minds), mysticism, and transcendentalism. However, I have come to realize the meaning of the adage to "bloom where you are planted" in that we can use the predominant religious instruction in the country that we are in to develop our spiritual essence. A lifetime of study would not exhaust the knowledge we can gain from a singular text. The Bible is not simply a static document written by a compilation of deceased authors for a bygone time. It is a "living, breathing, and sustaining" Word that continues to feed the soul, guides our path, comforts our sorrows, eradicates our fears, and transforms our minds.

The chronology of Jesus' life within the Bible leaves us wanting for the non-recorded years from thirteen to thirty, but what we do know about Jesus is that He studied and taught from the Old Testament Scriptures. So Jesus shows by example the importance of having a religious foundation for spiritual development (R/S). The journey toward wholeness and arrival within the pure-heart realm is not haphazard. It is a deliberate investment within a religious structure to hone spiritual development. The pathway toward wholeness requires that we feed the body…feed the mind…feed the spirit. Knowledge + experience = Wisdom. Knowledge + Action = Enlightenment. Enlightened beings, (e.g., Christ, Buddha, Gandhi, King, Malcolm X, Mother Teresa, President Carter, etc.) have shown us the pathway to wholeness where they've exhibited great spiritual awareness, fortified by their own religious edification, and exemplified their spiritual awareness in selfless servitude of others as fully enlightened beings.

The enlightened historical exemplars mentioned above possess great brilliance with their lives continuing to illuminate a darkened path; however, it is important to note that there are countless, unceremoniously recognized representatives of God's Brilliant Light carrying candles. We've hungered for a relationship with God, setting our eyes upon Him. We feed off of God's Attributes (some are revealed in Apostle Paul's epistle enumerating the Fruit of the Spirit). As we consume these spiritual attributes of love, peace, joy, etc., it heals us from the emotional, psychological, physiological, sexual, financial, or relational wounds we've endured over the years. And, as we consume more and more of God's Fruit, our fears and insecurities vanquish. God's abiding Love frees us of our egocentric need to compete, compare or contrast ourselves with others. Our combined religious edification and spiritual advancement advance us to the pure-heart spiritual realm (*"For you are the God of my salvation; On You I will wait all day"*).

FEED THE SPIRIT

The first part of the therapeutic process is to accurately identify the problem to be addressed in therapy. The first part of the spiritual process is to identify where you rate yourself on the spiritual continuum from 0-100. Begin by assessing where you are within the religious/spiritual typology. Use the quadrants as a guide versus a definitive determination as to where you might be on the spiritual continuum. That is, I have seen atheist display loving kindness in a way I imagine Christ would display and the behaviors of hate groups would actually have them rated lower than the typology would suggest; however, the typology showcases the degree of awareness of religious/spiritual connection. The typology includes individuals who are: Non-religious/Non-spiritual (NR/NS), Religious/Non-spiritual (R/NS), Spiritual/Non-religious (S/NR), Religious/Spiritual (R/S).

Religious/Spiritual Typology

NR/NS	R/NS
- Atheis - Agnostic - Humanist **0-25**	- KKK - Neo Nazis - Cults **25-50**
S/NR	R/S
- Paganism - New Wave - Animism **50-75**	- Christianity - Judaism - Islam **75-100**

WHAT WE DON'T FEED DIES - WHAT WE DO FEED LIVES

Now in the morning, as He returned to the city, He was hungry. And seeing a fig tree by the road, He came to it and found nothing on it but leaves, and said to it, "Let no fruit grow on you ever again." Immediately the fig tree withered away.
Matthew 21:18-21 (NKJV)

I often wondered about the above biblical quote. Jesus, "The Messiah," "The Son of Man," "The Son of God," "The Prince of Peace," sees a tree, perhaps in full bloom but devoid of figs, He curses it and the tree dies. Obviously, Jesus was famished and seeking sustenance from a known food source but in finding none, curses that tree, and the tree dies. Is this a reaction that we find within an entitled child that doesn't get his or her way? Indeed, some adults experiencing failed expectations may resort to temper tantrums, and is this what we are seeing? Jesus' reaction seems a bit spiteful and not befitting of a humble servant, a man of peace. So, I scratched my head and tried to make sense of this parable. Later in the passage, Jesus goes on to say that if his disciples have faith and confidence (no doubt) that they, too, can do as He has done and even greater by commanding a *"mountain to plop itself into the sea."*

Wow, that is certainly bold faith but is there more to understanding this parable? It has occurred to me that there is a lesson of integrity in the above passage. The fig tree is a fruit-bearing source but it was devoid of figs. It represented something that it didn't produce. As a therapist and a spiritual sojourner, I am certainly aware that many of us are representing something to others and we're devoid of "fruit" when people come near enough to check us out. It is disconcerting hearing people speak of their faith and quickly abandon that faith when the slightest test comes along. I am not pointing a finger of blame here as we know how quickly the disciples in the presence of Christ abandoned their faith when a test was revealed. Consider Peter's valiant attempt to walk on water only to lose his faith in fairly short order.

The lesson I have gleaned from the above is that we all must strive to become and continue to be people of integrity. We ought to discern the type of persons that we would like to become but merely arriving at a particular juncture does not maintain our character unless we continue to bear fruit. The "fruit" we bear is a testament to others of the persons we are. Like Christ, others with Christ-consciousness (or even those devoid of Christ-consciousness), are approaching us for spiritual nourishment only to find that we may be a barren tree (merely posing that we have something substantive to offer). There are doctors compromising the health of patients through ignorance, expedience, or profit (consider the opioid epidemic where in some areas there have been more opioid prescriptions given out than there are people in the community). There are pastors lining their pockets and living large; having guilt-induced their parishioners to give more than they can ill-afford to give. And, there are therapists who will shine a bright light on the clients' pathway through the darkness but remain squeamish when the same light is cast upon us.

Recently, I took the opportunity to visit a local church with a sparse congregation in a rural, Southwestern Minnesota community. It was a quaint church with a rustic exterior and a tinge of mildew emanating from the lower levels of the red brick church or perhaps from the tattered hymnals randomly placed on the back of the pews. I am careful not to equate the size of a congregation as evidence of spiritual advancement by the pastor or its membership, as the masses can be misled or simply entertained with little spiritual progression taking place. Nevertheless, within moments of the pastor's sermon, it was clear why his congregation was so diminutive. In stereotypical fashion that causes many of us to winch when we see this style of ministry replicated on television or in movies, was of a finger-pointing, bible-clutching, demonstratively yelling pastor damning the congregation for its "moral transgressions, unrelenting sins, sexual immoralities, and demonic indulgences."

Hmmm? I asked myself, "What is the nature of fruit that this well-intentioned minister was trying to dispense upon the people?" This type of rhetoric appears to me, to be the "fig" that Jesus reached for to provide him with physical nourishment (which is analogous to the rest of us as "spiritual nourishment") but the minister's tree was barren. The church, by its mere presence, represents itself as a "House of God" where those who have been victimized by the world can seek comfort and solace. When I listen to clients who adamantly deny the existence of God or the notion that people even have a "spiritual essence" as a central component of what we are, the pastor's scathing rhetoric makes it easy for me to understand their denials. Heaping additional condemnation upon wounded and fragile souls steers people away from a Loving, Nurturing, and Supportive God.

As spiritual exemplars, we must be careful about how we wield our "power." Yes, we are influencers, often described as "light" in a "world of darkness," but our words of condemnation and contempt for others are not God inspiring or even godly. Those operating out of the "indifferent-heart" realm or "craving-heart" realm will likely refute what I've just written. The former sees God through a punitive lens. They either deny the existence of God or see a wrathful God, who is ever-poised to have His "wax hot anger" flow out upon the people. If that is the way we see God, no wonder the pastor described above spews condemnation from the pulpit. The latter realm (craving-heart) is egocentric and philosophical by nature. These sojourners view God through a lens of intellectualizing, analyzing, and rationalizing. Indeed, they have an inverse relationship with God by reducing God to their intellectual understanding, encapsulating God within a limited box that they can categorize and expound upon within their own range of knowledge.

The realm beyond the indifferent-heart and craving-heart realm is the "pure-heart" realm. This is the realm where God is "bigger" than we are (as well as the essence of what we are) and we defer to God's Wisdom to lead us on our path. *"The steps of a good man are ordered by the Lord, And He delights in his way"* (Psalms 37:23, NKJV). God's human representatives (e.g., Jesus, Mohammed, Buddha, Mother Theresa, Gandhi, King, etc.) are "bigger" than we are (in terms of their conscious spirituality and prominence but not their spiritual essence). They and others (some greatly known and others lessor known from history) or the myriad of unsung individuals in our families, worksites, and communities reside squarely within the pure-heart realm. This is an important revelation because many of us may discount the degree of our spiritual advancement when trying to compare ourselves to the notables mentioned above.

Nevertheless, there are many times when we are confessing the attainment of spiritual attributes that we are just not producing. The fruit of love requires a great deal from us. Indeed, it is the most important fruit there is but seemingly difficult to produce. Matthew wrote in referencing Jesus, *"' ou shall love the Lord your God with all your heart, with all your soul, and with all your mind'. This is the first and great commandment. And the second is like it: 'You shall love your neighbor as yourself.' On these two commandments hang all the Law and the Prophets"* (Matthew 22:37-40; NKJV). The commandment requires a total commitment to the concept of love in mind, heart, and soul. We must align fully and completely with the Ultimate. The overflow of that love is dispensed to our fellow sojourners as each of us journey back to that from which we came.

We intuitively understand the concept of love but we get hung up on the application. When love is professed but is not dispensed, it is akin to the fig tree bearing no fruit. Christ, "The Anointed One," sought physical nourishment from the fig tree and cursed the tree itself when it produced no fruit because the tree had no purpose or utility. It is not unlike the "poser" that is colloquially called, "ghetto-fabulous" sporting the "bling" of un-amassed wealth without two nickels to rub together. The barren fig tree consumes resources and looks appealing but it offers nothing. Many of us are living lives of selfish consumption while giving little to the world.

God's unyielding instruction is for us to be fruitful and multiply; which is the producing and dissemination of our spiritual fruit.

Christ represented this concept in another parable (Matthew 12:25) of a traveling master giving his servants five, two, and one talent (former currency of Romans and Greeks); each according to the servants' abilities. The first two servants invested what they had been given and doubled it for the master by the time he returned. The third, riddled with fear, buried his talent in the ground to return what was given to him back to the master when he returned. Of course, this incensed the master and he took from the least of the servants and gave it to the others. This is not unlike Christ's reaction to the fig tree that was destined to produce fruit and gave nothing. A common thread running through each of these New Testament parables harken back to Old Testament lore when God empowers us with choice (Genesis) and encourages us to choose life, *"...I have set before you life and death, blessing and cursing; therefore choose life, that both you and your descendants may live..."* (Deuteronomy, 30:19; NKJV).

Christ goes on to tell us in Matthew (12:33) that a *"tree is known by its fruit"*; therefore, as we are cultivating, producing, and multiplying our fruit, "what we don't feed dies and what we do feed lives." Each of us hungers for legitimate spiritual fruit in this world. We hunger for love because God is Love! We hunger for God's Loving Embrace and the opportunity to replicate this love in the lives of others. Love is the thing that truly matters, the ultimate blessing of what God grants; yet, with our distorted minds we hunger for illegitimate things like lust, fame, power, pride, excessive eating, drugs, alcohol, and the like. Ironically, in our distorted vision of what we are (humanistic vs. the rightful heirs of God), we can hunger for fear, doubt, misery, abuse, etc. Should you think that no human being will hunger for abuse, you have just not met people who have engaged within self-injurious behaviors where they'll take jagged glass, box cutters, knives, nails, or other sharp objects to rip at their flesh.

I can't tell you how many people I've encountered over the years of doing therapy that have legitimate hunger needs (i.e. love, validation, respect, etc.) but will feast and gorge on illegitimate consuming of self-denigration, devaluation, and subjugation. I have had both men and women, at the hands of each other, who have been shot, stabbed, choked, and beaten so savagely that hospitalization was necessary; yet, to return again and again to the same abusive perpetrator. Ask them, and both victim and abuser will attest a perverted "love" for one another that keeps them fused within an unhealthy union. A young woman came to me distraught by her relationship with a man she described as a "narcissist, liar, philanderer, etc." Everyone who loves her wants her to extricate herself from this toxic relationship but she asserts, "I'm addicted to him." I get it because drama-based relationships are fueled by the adrenaline that feels addictive but there is no love in addiction. Here again, *a tree is known by its fruit* and love cannot be produced with selfish (vs. selfless) motives.

The production of anything; whether it is, good/evil, life/death, and blessings/curses must be fed or each will die. If love is fed, derision, rancor, and hatred dies. If derision, rancor, or hatred is fed, love dies. If love is not fed, derision, rancor, and hatred grow unchecked. If derision, rancor, and hatred are not fed, there remains a space for love to bloom. A fragmented or deflated ego state is spiritually malnourished. It craves the attributes of God. I have seen that even those people who are within the realm of ignorance (indifferent-heart realm) and deny the existence of God, hunger for the attributes of God. What person, pragmatist, humanist, or atheist, doesn't hunger for the attributes of love? Even those with exclusionary notions (i.e. bigots, sexists, or racists), hunger for love within their like-minded exclusionary groups.

I've been amazed when illustrating on the whiteboard within a therapy session the spiritual differentiation scale and some clients will actually rate themselves at a 0 of 100! Of course, when I point out to them that a zero represents the personification of the evil exhibit by such historical characters like "The Butcher of Uganda," Idi Amin Dada who killed 100,000 to 500,000 people during his regime, Pol Pot associated with the Cambodia Killing Fields with 1-2 million deaths, or Adolf Hitler, exterminator of over six million Jews, and the likes of Mao Zedong (or Mao Tse-tung) credited for unifying China but also purging/eliminating 40 to 80 million people, they will back off of their self-rating as a zero.

However, they will still rate themselves quite low. They have lost a healthy vision of themselves and it is borne out in their behaviors. Inflicting mass murder on hundreds of thousands or millions of people would never enter into their minds but the deliberate withering of their souls they readily embrace.

The desire for love is apparent within the indifferent-heart realm. The "holes in their souls" and "wounds in their psyche" are self-evident. Their hunger for love, indeed all fruit of the spirit, is insatiable; although their hunger pursuit is vastly distorted in this realm due to their profound ignorance. Within the indifferent-heart realm, lust may be fed here but love cannot grow. Addictions, compulsions, and hedonism thrive in this realm but each is absent of love. A fragmented sense of self has no real vision of the Essence of God and if one doesn't know God one cannot produce the spiritual attributes (Fruit) of what God is. Whereas love is at the heart of those operating within the pure-heart realm, at the core of those operating within the indifferent-heart realm is fear. A fear response will always be to avoid what is feared (intimacy or love) or to attack it (intimacy or love). A young client of mine with a promiscuous past fears rejection and abandonment has allowed multiple men to enter into her in a vain attempted to acquired love and then chooses to attack herself by cutting to mask the emptiness she feels on the inside.

The pursuit of love in the craving-heart (humanistic) realm is filled with comparisons, competitiveness, and contrasts. There is an over-functioning/under-functioning or insider/outsider dynamic within ego, residing in the craving-heart realm that relishes this imbalance. Notions of equality become nullified and ego demands the distinction as to whether we are in lofty or lowly places. Christians are not immune from setting up these hierarchical divisions and exclusionary camps where some reign supreme and others are left out. It was disheartening to see that this wealthy and largely Christian country not only endorse policies to close its borders to those fleeing abject poverty, persecutions, and gang violence but to separate family members and cage children. I've witnessed white and even black ministers engaging in exclusionary rhetoric and endorse policies (and/or politicians) that are grossly inconsistent with Jesus' Sermon on the Mount.

Nevertheless, in the craving-heart realm (which occupies the middle third on the spiritual differentiation scale), the notion of love and the mate selection process is based upon ego-centric needs; whether those needs place one at the top or bottom of the relationship hierarchy. Within dysfunctional relationships, people attempt to level one another, to bring the other down a notch and this can occur in the craving-heart realm. The inequities or imbalance occurring within this realm are not always perceived as contentious. The under-functioning person attaches to the over-functioning person with a vicarious heightening of his/her own status. Without equal desire, effort or accomplishment, the under-functioning person can bask in the glow of the over-functioners' accomplished goals, efforts, and achievements. The spouse of a minister, politician or doctor has unmerited favor and status based exclusively on their union with the over-functioning partner.

The over-functioner may initially value this complimentary style relationship because it stokes his or her notions of superiority; however, the imbalance creates the potential for conflict, emotional distance, and/ or cutoffs. Ego vies for distinction, separation, and power differentials; thereby, reinforcing the dominant character traits in the craving-heart realm of comparison, contrast, and competition. In doing so, we may falsely put forth images of ourselves that are indicative of the barren fig tree. This is the realm that the religious elite (e.g., Pharisees, Sadducees, Sanhedrin, etc.) reveled in their elite positions and felt threatened by the appeal of Jesus; thus, conspired to kill him. Interestingly, the over-fuctioner or elitist doesn't feel totally secure in their superiority, with the constant fear of being toppled by the oppressed.

Our adherence to ego in the craving-heart realm can certainly cause us to engage within egregious behaviors that reinforce separation that can lead to death but the capacity to recognize the "humanness" of other human beings tend to promote more benign contrast, comparisons, and competition with others. After all, it is the competitive nature of human beings that this country was founded and undergirded by capitalism. We relish our sports leagues and individual athletes that represent us throughout the world. Their achievements become our pride with a symbiotic relationship between performer and fan. In this realm, who doesn't want their achievements, status, prestige, or income to outshine those of others?

The competitive nature of human beings have explored the depths of the ocean, had men walk on the moon and launch unmanned rocket missions to the far reaches of our galaxy. Our competitive human nature will rapidly produce a vaccine for this dreaded COVID-19 virus ravishing the world; while at the same time this competitive nature artificially inflates the cost of life saving medications to satisfy the self-interests of greedy stockholders. Ironically, white collar corporate greed resulting in the death of others rarely result in murder charges or convictions, while the attempts of the indigent or minorities "trying to get over" with actions resulting in death is met with the ire of a punitive community that would like to see them "under the jail."

Love in the pure-heart realm is the purist form of love. Actually, it is the only realm which love can exist. It is not just the appearance of something good but also the produce of what the tree represents. The pure-heart realm is where all spiritual fruit ripens to maturity and is ready to be harvested and dispensed by all sentient beings. Love recognizes the mutuality and equality of all human beings. Love in the pure-heart realm raises our consciousness level to see ourselves within the most disregard and discarded members of our society. Those in the indifferent-heart realm have fused relationships with distorted notions of wholeness; thus, distorted perceptions of love. Those in the craving-heart realm will love with the expectation of being loved back. Nevertheless, those in the pure-heart realm have a higher duty and requirement for love. Luke, in recording the words of Christ, wrote, *"… [I]f you love those who love you, what credit is that to you? For even sinners love those who love them"* (6:32, NKJV). And further, Christ instructs us to *"… [L]ove your enemies, do good, and lend, hoping for nothing in return; and your reward will be great, and you will be sons of the Most High. For He is kind to the unthankful and evil. Therefore be merciful, just as your Father also is merciful"* (Luke, 6:35-36, NKJV).

Our placement on the spiritual continuum is contingent upon our spiritual development. Unlike our physical development that is independent of our psychological and spiritual development, we have to have the awareness of spirit to advance upon the spiritual differentiation scale. Within our physical being, nature automatically advances one to maturity and entropy. That is, we don't have to think about infancy or to advance ourselves spiritually to transition to adolescence. Nor does our thinking or spiritual awareness impede or advance us into adulthood. Nature has fully prepared the way for our physical beginnings, mid-phases and endings. Because of nature, physical life begins. Because of nature, the physical body matures into adulthood. Because of nature, entropy will transition animate matter into inanimate dust.

The brain is a physical organ and a product of nature; thus, in need of the sustenance from nature to form and develop. However, cognitively, our intellectual capacity is developed by our purposeful efforts. Throughout the world there are educational systems in place for rudimentary intellectual development; along with higher learning institutions to help facilitate critical thinking skills to apply this learning. With repetition, we are basically "exercising the brain" (or our cognitive capacity) with symbols, concepts and formulas to build upon foundational knowledge that makes us "smarter." We don't get "smarter" if we don't put our brain to task without "reading, writing and arithmetic" (or experiential learning). We are feeding and exercising the brain with knowledge and witnessing how this knowledge is played out in our day-to-day lives to develop wisdom.

Likewise, we develop our spirit by feeding and exercising the spirit. Of course, there are physical, intellectual and spiritual prodigies who ascend to the top of their development with little effort but for the vast majority of us, the arrival within the pure-heart spiritual realm is not an automatic process. While the forces of nature that push us along despite our intention, direction or effort, spirituality remains stagnant unless we are deliberately feeding it with spiritual sustenance and exercising (practice) it. I wrote about methods to develop (feed) the spirit in "The Fruit of the Spirit: A Primer for Spiritual Minded Social Workers" that include prayer, meditation, communion with God, study, etc. Awareness moves us out of the indifferent-heart realm but it is the awareness along with effort (practice) that keeps us in the pure-heart realm. Strength (physically speaking), cognition (mentally speaking), and spirituality will atrophy and regress if appropriate nourishment and sustained effort are not applied.

To reiterate the above, a child will develop into adulthood through the effects of nature independent of cognition and spiritual awareness. Wisdom and spiritual development is contingent upon our purposeful efforts. The spirit will direct our path and the mind develops a strategic plan to honor the direction of the spirit. The spirit can become malnourished if not fed properly or atrophy if not exercised regularly. The Apostle Paul warns us of this within his letter to the Galatians to *"...not grow weary while doing good, for in due season we shall reap if we don't lose heart."* (Galatians, 6:9; NKJV) (By the way, I've maintained that "goodness," as a fruit of the spirit, is a standard of conduct which we aspire toward.)

FEEDING THE SPIRIT

Each and every human being has legitimate hunger needs. We need love, respect, validation, appreciation, etc. When legitimate needs are not met, we feed on our illegitimate wants. Take some time to ascertain what your legitimate needs are. Legitimate needs are physiological, emotional, psychological, or spiritual needs that every human being needs; whereas, when we consume illegitimately (filling in that "hole in our soul") it is often hedonistic and self-indulgent. That is, food is a legitimate physiological need for every human being; whereas, caviar is an illegitimate desire that we could do without.

- Generate a list of the legitimate hunger needs that you have (i.e. love, validation, affection, respect, etc.)
- Determine if your list is a genuine hunger need or illegitimate (i.e. respect is a legitimate hunger need while craving for a winning lottery ticket is not).

- Examine your illegitimate desires to determine if it is due to a void within your legitimate needs (i.e., Is your illegitimate desire for alcohol used for liquid courage to allow you to engage socially for your legitimate acceptance needs)?
- Develop a plan that will help you obtain your legitimate needs (i.e. instead of searching for artificial, intoxicated connections at the bar, make a plan to volunteer service to elderly, neighbors, children, or others).

THE CHOSEN PEOPLE

For you are a holy people to the Lord your God, and the Lord has chosen you to be people for Himself, a special treasure above all the peoples who are on the face of the earth.
Deuteronomy, 14:2 (NKJV)

In the late 1960s there was a comedy sketch, musical entertainment show called, "The Smother Brothers Comedy Hour." The two brothers would play instruments and sing but also exchanged quips with one another. Tommy, the older of the two brothers, would constantly lament that their mom always loved the younger brother, Dick, the best. The audience roared with laughter, delighted by the sibling banter and the deniable truth that their parents favored one child over another. Of course, loving parents would never admit that they love or have chosen one child over the other but children know. My sister, the only girl in a brood of boys, was highly favored; even among our grandparents. I recall, out of spitefulness and envy, I took from my sister the handful of coins that my grandmother gave only to my sister and buried it in the yard. So, if anyone out there has a perennial blooming money tree growing in their back yard… "You're welcome."

Within our limited human capacity, it is easy to see why we might be a bit selective in our relationship choices but even within our familial and/or household connections we are still making choices and granting favor. A child who shares our interests, philosophies, and activities, we are inclined to gravitate toward. If we are ardent sports fans, we may consciously (or subconsciously) devote greater time and attention to the child that shares this passion versus the one that relishes ballet. Or, we may lavish more

28

attention to the child that is passionate for ballet because either he or she has greater affection for us than the one that values sports. A myriad of factors come into play when humans are choosing others in their lives and favoring one over another, but what about God? Are there chosen people for God?

Though it is hard to fathom the notion that there are "chosen people" the answer to the above question is "Yes!" Whether God chooses one religion over another is quite another thing. Consider this, that spirituality is God-made, as our spiritual essence is aligned with God (i.e. an awareness of, relationship with, and exemplifying within our walk with God). Religion is man-made (i.e. a set of tenants, rituals, and edicts) to coax humanity into choosing God over one's hedonistic/egocentric self. There are over 4000 different religions in the world and if we just carved out only one of those 4000+ religions, Christianity, there are over 34,000 Christian groups or denominations. In some ways, no matter how we "slice and dice" the enormity of this religious expression, there is a hunger for a spiritual connectedness for an Ultimate God or Greater Essence beyond ourselves.

Therein lies the good news. Our spiritual essence needs to be immersed in God just like our physical essence needs air to breathe. Of course, our human essence, endowed by ego, with a penchant for rationalization and separation, "wants" to have a myriad of religious expressions to convey a hierarchical notion that our God is better than your God. Or, more precisely, my way of connecting with God is superior to your way of connecting with God. We, humans, are nothing if not logical; thus, if my religious expression is greater than yours, yours must be wrong! We squabble over religion and miss the importance of our spiritual development. Jesus was never a "Christian" (as it is the followers of Christ called, "Christians") and I would dare say that the lineage to Christ that flowed through Abraham does not make Christ Jewish (as Abraham is the patriarch of Abrahamic religions including Judaism, Christianity and Islam and the term Israeli stems from Jacob's name change). Jacob's name (the "trickster") was changed to Israel ("one who wrestles with God") who is the progenitor of 12 offspring (12 tribes of Israel) with the reference of Jew as a derivative of Judah. It is Joseph (from the tribe of Judah) that follows the lineage of

Abraham, Jacob, David, etc. and not Mary (Immaculate Conception), so is the "Son of God" a Jew in the lineage of David?

Bishop Ussher, a 17th Century Theologian, calculated the creation of the world dates back to 4004 BC. A crude estimation of Abraham's life began approximately 2000 years after the creation (2056 BCE-1881 BCE). Abraham is the patriarch of God's chosen people but God chose Noah prior to Abraham and Adam prior to Noah. Adam's original sin separated humanity from its direct fellowship with God. Ironically, this "sin" (disobedience or turning one's back on God) was necessary to begin a life journey of choice. We have to have the knowledge of "good" and "evil" to have the ability to authentically choose. Adam, the first human creation from God, may have defied God but never really had to choose God. The descendants of Adam, instilled with knowledge of "good and evil" "blessings and curses," could now freely choose their path on this earthly plane.

Consider the plight of Adam and Eve's first two offspring (Cain and Abel). Abel's offering was received; thus, favored by God, and Cain's offering was rejected (disfavored by God). The sting of rejection for those living in the indifferent-heart realm can have severe repercussions as witnessed by Cain's murder of Abel. This is the same type of behavior we witnessed from a murderous perpetrator whose partner opts to leave. God knew Cain's heart and He could not choose Cain because Cain hadn't chosen Him. A relationship is a partnership of each choosing the other and God will always choose those who choose Him (but we must choose Him). Cain had knowledge of God and spoke to God but if he had "chosen" God (arriving in the pure-heart realm), Cain's disappointment would have never allowed him to kill his brother. *"Am I my brother's keeper?"* Cain derisively asked of God, knowing what he has done to his brother. Cain's question flowed from the mouth of someone residing within the indifferent-heart realm because those residing in the pure-heart realm will shout a resounding "Yes! We are our brother's keeper (at least as revealed in our actions by not harming one another).

Humanity, within its infancy, tapping into its full array of sense receptors while experiencing the material world, goes haywire. Choice, in the hands of infants and within the state of ignorance makes terrible choices; thus, hedonistic indulgences caused people to sprint at full speed away from God. The spiritual fruit of "discipline" (or "self-control") devolves into debauchery and people give in to the works of the flesh. "Peaceful" coexistence is replaced with insurrection and chaos. The fruit of "patience" (waiting on God) is thwarted by childish impudence. Our "faith" in God is diminished or extinguished with our new allegiance that weds us to the material world. God longs for us to choose Him but wickedness enveloped the earth and God's design was initially derailed with few people entering into the pure-heart realm. The remedy for this was a "do-over" with a flood washing clean the iniquities of our imprudent choices.

Following the great flood, the world needed to be repopulated. One would think that when people experience the enormity of a world-defining event, the generations that follow would have humbly devoted their lives to God. However, people have short memories and a sin-nature resumed choices endorsing worldly pursuits. Stemming from this horrific event of the "heavens opening" up and unleashing unrelenting rain for forty days and nights greatly impacts the psyche of survivors. Whether one believes himself to be favored or not, what is the impact upon the psyche when everything known was wiped out? A trauma response has Noah lying naked in his tent from a drunken stupor and with his reactive shame placing a curse upon his son, Ham, for discovering his father's nakedness.

If nothing else, Ham, Shem and Japheth (Noah's sons) were prolific and did their part in repopulating the world. The Bible doesn't reveal a lot of information between the time of Noah and the arrival of Abraham but it is interesting to note that even though Noah and his immediate family was chosen to survive the destruction of the world, Noah is not considered the Father of all Nations nor was his family dubbed, "the chosen people." The descendants of Adam, empowered with the "knowledge of good and evil" choose indulgence within the material world over God, but also, the trauma-induced descendants of Noah were clearly residing in the indifferent-heart realm. God can't catch a break, in that we've let Him down when given everything in the Garden and then once again when He attempts a do over with the flood.

There is a recalcitrant nature within people who don't wear masks during a pandemic, who fight therapists for their own healing, or those who defy the wisdom of He who has created us. When I consider that many of the clients I have served have multiple generations of trauma and impacted by toxic shame that plays havoc in their present lives, I can see how the results of a "world-ending" event moves people away from God and those people indulging a hedonistic self. Sodom and Gomorra was just a couple of examples of the world's "wickedness and depravity." People, en masse, have turned away from God with a mixture of debauchery, idolatry, and polytheism. Indeed, God instructed Abraham to get away from his own people who have lost their way so that Abraham was not corrupted by their influence. Abraham wouldn't have gone anywhere if his passion was in his people and his faith was in the familiar.

So, the "chosen people" is not God choosing one group of people over another (per se) but it is us choosing God! Abraham was considered righteous not by his behaviors but by his faith. Abraham was far from perfect but he did choose God. Apostle Paul conveys in his epistle to Galatians 3:6 (NKJV), *"...Abraham 'believed God, and it was accounted to him for righteousness."* Those residing within the indifferent-heart realm cannot choose God, even if they express that they do. It is like the bigot who asserts that she can't be a bigot because she has "minority" friends (meaning that she is "friendly" to the token minority at work) but would disown her daughter if she opted to marry someone from a minority group. One cannot choose God and endorse politicians or religious leaders that sanction the imprisonment of immigrant children and have not learned the lesson that we are indeed our brothers' keepers.

A relationship or covenant with God (or anyone else) is akin to a business transaction (contract). For any contract to be legitimate there must be a discussion about the parameters, a "meeting of the minds" with an agreement of the terms, and a degree of equity (mutual benefit) between the parties. If one is a child, the minor cannot enter into a business arrangement. If someone is inebriated, she cannot be held to a contract made within an inebriated state. If the person is mentally incapacitated, he does not have the wherewithal to engage within a contract. A friendship has similar transactional exchanges in order to be called a "friendship." A friendship requires knowledge of the person. This knowing will take an investment in "intimacy" (which I equate with the "sharing of one's souls"). A friendship requires trust/fidelity (which generates a space of safety to allow for vulnerability). A friendship is caring for the other (which means we must know and trust the other to adequately care for the other).

A one-sided pursuit of a relationship may be considered an infatuation or "stalking" but it is not a friendship. There is no mutuality; thus, if there is a "relationship contract" in place, it must be voided. God has chosen humanity because He has created humanity but we must equally choose God. God will not "stalk" us or force us into accepting Him. *"Ask, and it will be given to you; seek, and you will find; knock, and it will be opened to you"* (Matthew, 7:7; NKJV). So when Abraham and the descendants of Abraham choose a Monolithic God, a "covenant" or "contract" is in place. A breach in the contract voids the contract, but the breach is always on our end. Nevertheless, there is a cost to us (not to God) for us breaking the contract with Him. Of course, there is tremendous leniency because God forgives constantly and will renew our contract again and again but disfellowship from God is darkness. Life choices made in darkness reinforce our ignorance.

Choosing God does happen in the craving-heart realm but this realm is fraught with ego; thus, we may oscillate between choosing God and choosing ourselves. God can be reduced down to being the instrument of humanity. We are arrogantly running the show and beseech God's intercession when things go off the rails. Ego (easing God out) intellectualizes, rationalizes, and analyzes the empirical world with God as an afterthought. When we can't figure it out for ourselves or when we are in deep despair, we cry out to God. Nevertheless, in this realm, God still shows up; only that we are using God versus God using us. This position is not endemic to God but is replicated in therapy settings where clients come in with self-diagnoses and self-treatment regimens. I doubt if I ever really convinced an ardent client that marijuana is a drug and their mental health is compromised by the substances they choose to ingest.

In the pure-heart realm, the transactional relationship results in a fuller and more complete relationship with God. We are in partnership or collaboration with God. We yield to God's Wisdom, fueled by His Love and we walk in undeniable faith. None of the Biblical heroes were perfect. Indeed, they all were flawed. Moses, David, Saul, Paul, Ezekiel, Peter, Noah, whoever is named we can see their flaws. Likewise, you and I are flawed. We are caught between our sin nature and godly pursuits. Again, it is not an allusive pathway to perfection that matters, it is the relationship we have with God that matters. Whether it is Abraham whose "righteousness was credited by his faith" or David, "a man after God's own heart," we are talking about the strength of the Covenant relationship versus honing ourselves into perfection.

So, to be clear, in referencing "God's chosen people," God chooses everyone! He is not a "respecter of people" (paraphrasing Paul in Romans 2:10). He is not choosing a race, gender, social-economic status (SES), political affiliation, geographic locations, or religion. Not unlike the father within the biblical story of the prodigal son, God chooses the son that leaves and foolishly engages the world and the son that stays and is envious of his brother's return. God chooses us! He chooses you and he chooses me. Are we choosing God? *"For those who live according to the flesh set their minds on the things of the flesh, but those who live according to the Spirit, the things of the Spirit"* (Romans 8:5; NKJV).

If God chooses everyone, what about the dichotomous statements throughout the Bible emphasizing heaven and hell, good and bad, righteousness and evil or the chosen and nonchosen? Even Christ talked about separating the wheat from the shaft or sheep from goats, so there has got to be clear delineating lines of demarcation separating one group from another, doesn't it? The Bible and other divinely written and godly inspired books are merely manuals on how to be spiritual in a material world. Those manuals point us in the direction of God and reveal the consequence of those residing in darkness. There is no compass, map or manual necessary for the one who arrives home. The purity or goodness of God that resides within each and every one of us is revealed when we shed our human and flawed nature to re-immerse within the spiritual Oneness of the Ultimate God.

The gift of our human experience God allows us freedom…the autonomy to choose the type of experience we will have on this earthly plane. There are many terrible choices that many of us choose when we haven't arrived into the pure-heart realm. How does one choose methamphetamines, alcohol, prostitution, affairs, stealing or any such behavior unless lost in the indifferent-heart realm? Think about the demon-possessed man that no chains could bind, injuring himself and raging against others that Christ exorcised the demonic spirits (legion) from the man into pigs (Matthew 5). Whether possessed, mentally ill or drug-induced, the deranged man was lost within the indifferent-heart realm but reclaimed by Christ. There was nothing anyone else could do but Christ reached out to free him and grant the man peace.

Like the possessed man, so many people are hurting (thus hurting themselves and others), lost and residing in a realm of ignorance. Women (and men) that sacrifice their peace and sanity choosing to return again and again to an abusive partner have lost their way. The compulsive indulgences within alcohol, gambling or porn stems from those who do not know themselves or know God. Those who are paralyzed with fear and explosive with rage don't know God. Their ignorance is profound but the genesis of their ignorance is rarely (if ever) their fault. No one asks for ignorance but people make choices out of ignorance. As a therapist, who is privy to the stories of those inflicted with egregious, inhumane neglect and/or abuse and they mimic these egregious acts in the behaviors they choose, I bear no harsh judgment of them.

People don't typically choose the perpetuation of their ignorance. They truly don't know that they don't know. All of us are on a developmental spiritual pathway that starts in ignorance of not knowing ourselves but we are advancing toward awareness and enlightenment (knowledge plus action) but this natural process is disrupted significantly when our spirit/

psyche is wounded, fractured, or broken. Just like the addict or alcoholic chooses his or her drug of choice or favorite alcoholic beverage; neither has chosen to be an addict or alcoholic. The diabetic may choose the type of foods to eat or not eat but no one chooses diabetes. Many will choose the type of impulsive or compulsive behaviors that keep them trapped in the indifferent-heart realm but no one willfully chooses ignorance.

A child, within his or her own ignorance, witnessing a defecating dog eat its own feces, decides to try it, does the shocked parent disown the child? It is incredibly gross and not what you've taught the child, so should you just cut that child off? What about the defiant adolescent who sneaks into your purse in the middle of the night and takes the keys to the car that you've explicitly stated that she couldn't drive, do you wash your hands of her? How about the 18-year-old boy, who thinks he is a man, curses you to your face and takes off for three years with absolutely no contact with you and then resurfaces, is there any forgiveness for those behaviors? The ignorance on the part of a child at any age is not a death knell to our love and we never cut off from them.

God cannot choose us if we haven't chosen him on this earthly plane. Thus, the pathway of our journey, replete with blessings or curses is our choice to make. Nevertheless, at the end of this physical journey, God's "arms" are wide open longing for our spiritual embrace and welcome home! There is no penance or penalty due because the purity of spirit is devoid of our human foibles or flaws. I inform clients that come to me with great shame about who they are and guilt about what they've done that at the beginning stages of our spiritual development is a deflated or fragmented ego state. This deflation or fragmentation of self is a distortion of ourselves based upon our ignorance. The reason distortions are based on ignorance because all distortions are lies!

FEEDING THE SPIRIT

At birth, and even prior to birth, many people have experienced physiological insults. A pregnant, Nigerian mother, impacted by famine and war, unable to be well-nourished, visit an OB-GYN doctor, or take prenatal vitamins, unintentionally creates physiological insults to her unborn fetus. Likewise, an illegal substance-using, pregnant woman in the United States contributes to the physiological insults to her unborn child. Physiological wounds, psychological wounds, emotional wounds, spiritual wounds, and the like are causal factors for a fragmented ego state (psyche). What wounds do you carry (e.g., familial, sexual, financial, interpersonal, educational, vocational)? With "newer" therapy approaches [e.g. Eye Movement Desensitization Reprocessing (EMDR), Emotional Freedom Technique (EFT), Accelerated Resolution Therapy (ART), etc.] the effects of trauma can be healed without excavating or reliving the trauma. However, with traditional or spiritual approaches, you'll still need to do the excavating and healing work. Feeding the spirit requires us to repair earlier trauma and this starts in recognizing what traumas we've been impacted by. Implement the below process to determine what wounds you are suffering from and march toward healing. In this exercise, avoid the causes of your wounds but examine the impact. Get out your journal and examine the following:

Psychological/Emotional

- What cognitive distortions do you have (e.g. catastrophizing, generalization, black and white thinking, etc.)? What is your worldview? How do your core beliefs adversely impact your life? How are your thoughts feeding your higher self? How are your thoughts reinforcing notions of a lower self? - What emotions do you have trouble feeling? What emotions do you feel too much? How are your emotions impacting your life (emotion dysregulation)? How are your emotions contributing to your capacity as a spiritual being to have a human experience? Are you using your emotional array effectively to advance spiritual progress or are you remaining fused within emotional reactivity?

Spiritual

- What spiritual wounds do you harbor? Have you lost faith in God? How does your fractured faith adversely impact your life? If your spiritual reservoir has been depleted, how can you replenish yourself without plugging back into your Source? How have your spiritual ruptures altered your peace, joy, love, etc.?

Behavioral

- How are you conducting yourself privately? How are you conducting yourself publically? What compulsive behaviors are you engaged within (e.g., drinking, drugs, sexually acting out, unlawful activities, etc.? What aspirational goals do you have? What behavioral steps can you implement daily to achieve those goals? Do your behavioral responses comport with your moral essence that is aligned with your notions of God? Does your behavior contribute to your overall healing or are you remaining stuck in the reactivity related to your trauma?

THEY SAY...

He who is slow to anger is better than the mighty, and he who rules his spirit than he who takes a city.
Proverbs 16:32 (NKJV)

They say (and I have no idea who "they" are) that "those who can do, do and those who cannot do, teach." They say that "people go into ministry to work through the demons that plagued their own lives." They say that "people become therapists to work through their own psychological issues and specialize in the areas they need the most help with." So, as a former educator, informal minister, and current therapist, I am undoubtedly pretty messed up! At least, that is what "they say." However, if there is an ounce of truth to the above, I've pondered how I have become the "anger management specialist" at my agency?

The truth is, I never volunteered to run the anger management therapy group. I was assigned to facilitate the group and I was likely assigned because I was the "newbie" at the agency, charged to facilitate the group that no one else wanted to do. After all, who wants to work with recalcitrant, antagonistic, court-referred clients? Nevertheless, we are spiritually conscripted to work out things (whether interpersonal or intra-psychological) to advance upon our spiritual path, thus my foray into the anger management group as the facilitator netted reciprocal results. Namely, therapy is a co-evolutional journey, in that therapists guiding clients to wholeness are also marching toward wholeness. Facilitating the group gave me the opportunity to reflect on the concept of anger and its relationship to spirituality.

That is, agitation and worry, fear and doubt, indulgence within sense desires, sloth and torpor; along with irritation and anger are all impediments to spiritual advancement. However, I then started wrestling with the notion that so many spiritual exemplars in the Bible displayed anger. I have learned and taught that anger derives from a sense of threat to safety and response for protection. I tell my clients that I am conflicted here because every human being has the right to self-preservation. Indeed, every animal has the right to self-preservation. I am not prepared to tell people that when someone kicks your door in to threaten you or your family, or if you are accosted on the streets that you don't have a right to self-preservation, even to the point of ending the life of the perpetrator. How do I uproot a man's perception of his role of protector and even the woman's role as a "mama bear" to protect their own? I acknowledge my own lack of spiritual differentiation when I stand ready to offer up a vigorous defense if I, a loved one, or even a stranger was in jeopardy.

Some will assert that anger is justified for protection and safety and it is represented by people like Peter. Peter was often thought of as a "hothead" (though interesting, the disciple in which Christ built his church), rose up in what he thought to be righteous anger in cutting off the ear of a sentry attempting to arrest Christ. He was in the presence of Christ, learning about love, forgiveness, and turning the other cheek but when the notion of safety and protection became real, Peter went on offense. Nevertheless, Christ didn't mount a defense based upon anger or violence. When we examine the lives of every legitimate spiritual exemplar whose safety was in jeopardy have not used violence for their own safety or the protection of others.

Anger results from frustration and impotence. Let's look at Moses. He was chosen to be the emancipator of the Israeli people who were subjugated to generations of servitude, flares up in anger to kill an Egyptian overseer, and fled prosecution. He didn't have an authentic knowledge of God when he acted out; thus, we can forgive the transgressions of the ignorant. However, he spent 40 years in the wilderness forging a new identity and relationship with God, becoming a main progenitor of Judaism and subsequently Christianity and Islam. Moses, this man of God, has such an unique relationship with God that he becomes transfigured in the presence of God, but somehow, he loses his cool, feeling frustrated by the antics of the people worshiping idols in his absence, and tosses down the very words of God carved into stone. I get it, Moses, I get it. You are working hard on behalf of the people and in short order, they manifested doubt and engaged their sense desires by making an idol. This is akin to how a therapist might feel when laying out an exquisite plan for client empowerment who abdicates the plan to return to the misery he or she is familiar with.

Anger stems from the feelings of betrayal and humiliation and there is no greater character in the Bible to illustrate this than Samson. Samson was smitten by Delilah. Here again, we see how indulgence in our sense desires diverts us from our spiritual path. Delilah starts off in the Bible as a woman of ill-repute ("harlot") but is also a Philistine, which the Israelis' were at odds with. Samson chose lust over the Lord and paid the price with betrayal, stripped of power, eyes gouged out and tied to the temple pillars with his humiliation on full display. By way of an appeal to God and a final burst of anger, Samson brings down the temple.

Anger was manifested in Noah's shame (lying naked in his tent from a drunken stupor), Saul's pride (trying to kill David), and even from Christ with His feelings of disrespect (moneychangers in the temple). Preeminent Biblical characters have displayed anger which may normalize for the reader that anger is a byproduct of spiritual beings; however, anger is a fetter that binds us to our human nature and is the antithesis of our spiritual essence. Internalized anger is depression and externalized anger is rage. Anger short circuits our reason and disrupts our calm. Anger corrodes our spirit and derails our journey on our spiritual path. Anger does not propel us forward; it pushes us backward. When anger becomes the impetus for action, the action will often be ill-considered.

Christ is fully divine and was fully human. Like each of us who have been given this gift of a human experience, Christ was endowed with every human emotion. He has experienced anger, fear, doubt, worry, irritation, frustration, the whole gamut. It was important for Jesus to have had this human experience, to become a bona fide exemplar leading the way. I don't believe that one has to be down in a pit in order to lift another person out but "they say" that one has greater credibility who has fallen and risen than some elitist, moralistic being dictating a path for others that they have not gone down.

Anger, like any and all of our human emotions, ought to be experienced and felt. Anger, like any and all of our human emotions, can be informative and instructive. Anger, like any and all human emotions, should not be held on to or hoarded. Anger can be informative and instructive in that it lets us know that a boundary has been crossed. Anger, like any and all of our human emotions, gives us an opportunity to dive deep and discover more about ourselves. When anger arises, we have the opportunity to ask each of the process questions to be informed and create an instructive plan to move forward. We may ask, "Who is making me angry?" Is it others or my perceived reaction to others? "What is making me angry?" Is it the situation or my reaction to the situation? When am I feeling anger? Is it mornings, evenings, tired, hungry? Where am I feeling anger? Is it internal (i.e., gut, shoulders, head, etc.) or external (i.e., in traffic, work, or at home)? Why is this making me angry? Is it due to underlining emotions of sadness, hurt, embarrassment, etc.? How am I handling my anger? Is it constructive; therefore, facilitating greater connections, or is it destructive by creating hurt and harm?

Anger, like any and all of our human emotions, will come to us (perhaps unannounced) allowing us to experience the sensation of the emotion but then we must let it go. Hanging on to anger creates bitterness, resentments, and hatred. Anger, like any and all of our emotions, should flow through us unimpeded and unobstructed as the flow of electricity comes in from one side of the outlet to animate our devices and returns to the ground. A kink in the cord may disrupt the flow and become a risk for fire; while a surge of electricity without discharge can destroy our electrical device. Indeed, all emotions should flow through us unimpeded and unobstructed, as even pleasant emotions like calm may make us sedate and forego necessary action. Clients who are engaged in daily cannabis consumption heralds the calm of their experience; whereas, observers decry their lack of motivation and industry.

I admire the historical exemplars of King, Gandhi, or Jesus who have advanced significantly in their spiritual progression that wouldn't advocate (as I have) to group members struggling with anger management their right to self-preservation. However, I wouldn't be truthful to pretend that I was there. I realize that retaining anger grants greater credence in the material world versus granting credence to God. Intellectually, I know that anger is often the reactive entitlement of the uninitiated (spiritually ignorant), devoid of even rational discernment. If I rise up in anger and blow away my big toe with a shotgun because I didn't like the way it looked or was otherwise bothering me at the time, I am not demonstrating the spiritual wisdom that I am capable of achieving.

"They say" that people who enter into the mental health field have issues to work through themselves and I recognize through my facilitation of the anger management group and more broadly as a therapist, I have work to do. In referencing the Proverb's quote at the top of this chapter, I do believe that I am slow to anger but I've yet to govern my spirit. After all, why else would I espouse the ego position of self-preservation versus a principled, Godly perspective of doing no harm to the group? "They say" it is progression and not perfection is our goal, so I'll keep working.

FEEDING THE SPIRIT

Anger and any disconfirming emotion that doesn't align with the essence of God must be erroneously fed if it is to grow. Likewise, spiritual calm must be cultivated if it is to grow. To cultivate spiritual calm and diminish anger happens with daily mindfulness. Focus upon the spiritual fruit of peace. Inhale peace. Exhale anger. Notice your calm and vanquishing anger.

SAY, WHAT?

When wisdom enters your heart, and knowledge is pleasant to your soul; Discretion will preserve you, understanding will keep you…
(Proverbs, 2:10-11; NKJV)

I was listening to a scholarly gentleman (whom I'll call, "John;" given that I can't remember who he was) make an astute statement that piqued my interest. He postulated that there is no way any of us can proclaim that a deity exists, the reason for our being, what we are here to do, or if there is an existence beyond our death. He went on to say that the mysteries of the universe are vast; thus, there is no way anyone can have a definitive answer. There was a cogent ring of truth in this speaker's statements, as I know it is the height of hubris to presume a singular claim can be the definitive statement about an ever-expanding universe and our understanding of God, our reason for being, purpose, and existence beyond death. This, of course, sparks ongoing tension and debate over rationalism and theism.

Rationalism stems from an epistemological (how we know what we know) shift in the 17th – 18th Centuries, during the Age of Enlightenment, promoting "reason" as the ultimate method in discerning truth. Theism, the belief in an unseen but highly involved creationist God waned in the minds of many with other complementary ways of knowing brought forth in the 1600's such as modernity/positivism, empiricism, scientific methods and the like took root. Fortunately, this Age of Enlightenment hasn't driven God completely out of business. If we endorse God (as I do) in the scientific discipline of psychology (though some argue that psychology is a pseudo-science), how do I reconcile my spiritual beliefs with the statements made in the previous paragraph and if I can't make a rational, definitive argument about "spirituality," why in the world should I be promoting this in psychology?

Do you remember the parable of the blind men touching different parts of the elephant coming to varying conclusions? Depending upon who tells the story, it is either three blind men or six. The trunk of the elephant and/or its tail is considered a snake. The elephant's massive leg is considered to be a tree. The girth of the elephant is considered a wall and so on. The principle of the parable is that all of us are blind in some way or the other, perceiving the essence of something, utilizing one sense (touch), and concluding that each has the truth. In like fashion, each of us argues the "rightness" of our position using varying ways of knowing and limited means of perceiving to bolster our dogmatic positions. With thousands of psychometric instruments, hundreds of psychological treatment options, and multiple theoretical orientations, I can acknowledge that my therapeutic approach comes from my own "blind touch of the elephant."

However, rationalism is not necessarily the antithesis of spirituality. Ok... ok...I hear your objections, to which I agree that rationalism is a logical approach to understanding truth; whereas, spirituality is diametrically opposite as a faith-based epistemology, but I'm going to take a stab at it. God or spirituality is not an appendage of the elephant that someone has ahold of and trying to make sense of it. God or spirituality is the elephant that all of these methods, theories, worldviews, etc. are trying to make sense of by grasping the various appendages of the elephant. Spirituality gives birth to rationalism, or modernity, or empiricism, but it is not the other way around. The Essence of God and Spirit makes all things possible but we cannot use the limitations of logic (rationalism) to comprehend the Essence of God. We cannot use the empirical measures of scientific methods that observe, measures, or counts reality to deduce the Essence of God; however, the ability to observe, measure, and count our physical reality is a result of the Spiritual Essence of God.

Our journey to wholeness is marginalized when we focus exclusively on the physical aspects of who we are (hedonism, materialism, carnality), or when we focus exclusively on the mental aspects of our humanness (intellectualizing, rationalizing, justifying). We must integrate the triune essence of ourselves to incorporate our physical and mental essence with our spiritual essence. Our spiritual essence connotes meaning, purpose, direction, and connection. As such, I refute the statements in the first paragraph that there is no way to proclaim a deity exists, the meaning of our existence, the purpose of our existence and the continuation of our existence.

Deist in the 1700's conflated spirituality with rationalism in recognizing reason over revelation discovering God in nature; yet, deemphasizing God's ongoing involvement in our lives. The spiritual measure that we must use to envision the entirety of the "elephant" (God or spirit) is faith. *"By faith we understand that the worlds were framed by the word of God, so that the things that were seen were not made of things that were visible"* (Hebrews 11:3; NKJV). Additionally, Paul writes in Romans, *"For in it* (the Gospel) *the righteousness of God is revealed from faith to faith; as it is written, 'The just shall live by faith.'"* (Romans 1:17; NKJV) So, we can't measure the Spirit of God with a ruler or view the Essence of God through a magnifying glass. We tap into faith to unveil our spiritual path because there is nothing concrete or tangible about the Fruit of the Spirit.

As I "clap back" against "John" with my spiritual measure of faith, I affirm the absolute existence of God! I assert that not only can we ascertain our meaning upon this earth, but it is also an imperative of our spirit. How we discern meaning from a spiritual and psychological point of view is determinative of the life we lead. The meaning of our existence is answering that existential question as to why we are here. "John" may not know and he may have never asked himself the question but there are discernable reasons for our existence. We are spiritual beings having a human experience with autonomy and freedom of choice. That is the gift that God has granted to each of us. The meaning of our existence from a psychological perspective is to forge healthy relationships, starting with a healthy, integrated, sense of self.

Meaning equates with our purpose in that we must first ascertain why we are here with our understanding of the meaning and what we are here to do for the purpose. Spirituality is also about discerning our direction, with clarity of vision to march in the direction of wholeness that aligns with the Essence of God. Of course, God grants us choice and we can gravitate toward darkness versus the light. The Light of God shines brightly, revealing faults, flaws, or blemishes as we move closer to the Light. Light is not shame-producing. It is healing, as we know that the best disinfectant is exposure to sunlight. To the contrary, it is our shameful behaviors that have us running toward the darkness in order to hide.

"When wisdom enters your hearts…," (which is knowledge plus experience) it comes from an abiding relationship with God, *"For when envy and self-seeking exist, confusion and every evil thing are there. But the wisdom from above is first pure, then peaceable, gentle, willing to yield, full of mercy and good fruits, without partiality and without hypocrisy. Now the fruit of righteousness is sown in peace by those who make peace"* (James 3:16-18; NKJV). We have to spend time knowing God and experiencing God to receive this wisdom. When we earnestly seek to know God, we favor this experience and are likewise favored by God. Intention and desire lead us to the pure-heart realm where our relationship with God is truly manifested.

James, disciple of Christ and brother of Jesus confirms that self-seeking (indifferent-heart realm) and envy (craving-heart realm) are both replete with confusion (ignorance) and every evil thing (the antithesis of God), "but the wisdom from above is first pure" (pure-heart realm), yielding all spiritual fruit for all those who seek God. The ways of knowing are enumerable in the material world but the way in knowing God is through faith. Apostle Paul asserts, *"So then faith comes by hearing, and hearing by the word of God"* (Romans 10:17; NKJV). Faith will reveal our understanding of God, our reason for being, purpose, and existence beyond death.

FEEDING THE SPIRIT

I wrote about within my book, "The Fruit of the Spirit" various ways to related with God and each of these are methods that we can use to build faith. I will reference them here with the hope that you'll establish your own method in building your faith: Meditation, prayer, communion, dialogue, study, contemplation, rituals, service and integration of self.

WANTS AND NEEDS

Delight thyself also in the LORD: and he shall
give thee the desires of thine heart.
Commit thy way unto the LORD; trust also in
him; and he shall bring it to pass.
(Psalms, 37:4-5; KJV)

I have encountered several people along my spiritual journey who have renounced the existence of God. On rare occasions has any of them started off with denial of God in their childhood and continued this denial throughout their adulthood. I don't mean to suggest that there are not those children subjected to unimaginable neglect and cruelty by primary care providers who are supposed to love them, who reject the notion of God. I don't mean to suggest that there are not those children indoctrinated within agnostic, atheistic, or indifferent-heart views who have shut off the notion that a loving, compassionate and generous God exists. I get it. We live what we learn; however, it is those who have been exposed to spiritual indoctrination in their childhood and have turned away in their adulthood, I find to be perplexing.

Well, perhaps it is only "somewhat perplexing." What I have found that those who have had an initial exposure to spirituality that didn't take "root" in their adulthood results from great disillusionment. Kids endorse the notion of fairy tales with innocence and glee. As children mature, even within their childhood, they come to realize that it is a family member versus a "tooth fairy" that deposits money underneath their pillow while sleeping. They come to understand that it can't be Santa Claus leaving presents for them on Christmas Eve because they don't have a chimney for Santa to slide down from. The Prince combing the kingdom to find Cinderella is realized as a little girl's fantasy and even if Peter Pan never grows up, children do discover Neverland never existed.

Having been fooled so frequently by loving family members and from the bulk of society that perpetuates fables, fairytales, and myths, the doubters are justified in their doubting but they can also point to great disillusionments in their lives that further bolster their doubt. Those doubters will tell me that they've had a fervent belief in God but God let them down. They've prayed incessantly for the amelioration of sickness within a family member but the person died. They were loyal workers at a company for years and petitioned God directly to advance him or her to the vacant management position; yet, the person who was selected was a recent hire, whom the overlooked employee has trained. They've prayed feverishly for their handful of lottery tickets to have one with the winning numbers; yet, someone they perceive as "undeserving" wins the prize. For them, if faith in God was ever really present, an unanswered prayer dashes it completely.

People have considered the wise words of David to *"Delight in the Lord and He will give you the desires of your heart"* and they winch at the notion that their desires are not being fulfilled. They have desired great celebrity, a mansion on the hill or a fancy car within the driveway that puts their neighbors to shame and none of these desires manifest. Perhaps others have petitions that are nobler in that they wish for world peace while dismayed by ever-increasing conflicts and wars; stability in a marriage that teeters toward divorce due to apathy or adultery; or that their children will escape the wrath of bullying within school, yet, he or she becomes the actual target. *"My God, my God, why have you forsaken me?"* When we take into account this explicit contract that David shares with us regarding God that if we just delight in Him and we'll receive the desires of our heart and we can't even muster enough money to have our favorite pizza delivered, something is wrong! Well, I agree. There is something amiss here.

Can it be that once we've actually chosen God He doesn't choose us? Of course not. The transactional relationship we have with God is not that if we "delight in Him" or "trust in Him," whatever our carnal flesh desires are we will obtain. However, when we "delight" ourselves in the spiritual essence of God and then all things aligned with "spirit" will be afforded to us. A home, a car or even our favorite pizza is not a "desire of the heart" that is aligned with God's Will. Our alignment with God versus mammon, changes the desires of our heart. *"When I was a child, I spake as a child, I understood as a child, I thought as a child: but when I became a man, I put away childish things."* (I Corinthians 13:11, KJV)

Those who have been exposed to their spirituality and the Essence of God within their childhood but loses their vision of spirituality or relationship with God in their adulthood are still hanging onto a "child's mentality." It is not unlike a "child's mentality" operating when we believed in Santa Claus or the Tooth Fairy; thereby abdicating all needs in favor of our wants. We don't have the wherewithal in our childish or adolescent mindset to know what our needs are; so our wants in the material world predominate, and the absence of those material desires disappoints us greatly. The denial of God granting our childish expectations triggers immediate reactivity; thereby, renouncing the existence and/or sovereignty of a Divine Spiritual Being. Consider the transactional relationships human parents have with their human children when favor (privilege) is typically tied in with obedience, maturity, and responsibility. A loving parent may assert that if you "delight" in me (i.e. understand and appreciate family standards/ values and obey these values and standards) the child can have the desires of his/her heart (e.g., iPhone, Gameboy, hanging out with friends) as long as they coincide with standards and values.

We can't expect a loving parent, who abhors the use of drugs; thereby, raising the child with these same values and standards, to condone the "desires of the heart" in the child who now pursues drugs. We cannot expect a Spiritual Entity who is the antithesis of the material world, to continually grant us access to the material world when He is trying to develop spiritual maturity within us. So when the doubter prays fervently for a job and doesn't get it, the job is irrelevant to God. God is not a respecter of human beings; thus, titles are meaningless for Him. A fancy home may stoke envy within family and friends but God knows that it will one day meet the fate of entropy and impermanence, only to be replaced by the incessant desire to obtain another home. The appetite for desires of the carnal world is never quenched by more things from the carnal world.

A true seeker of God, who "delights" in the Lord doesn't have the immature faith of one who indulges within the fantasy that all material indulgences will be fulfilled, but our alignment with God will grant us the desires of our hearts (to be more like God). We want to be more loving; even when confronted by impudence or abandonment. We seek to be more patient; even if we've lost it all. We want to augment our faith; even when our health is under assault or our source of income vanishes overnight. We want to hone gentleness and kindness; even with enemies surrounding us completely. We want to experience joy; even though our bank statement is at zero. We want to find peace in our minds, families, and communities; even though our peace may be under attack. We want to establish standards of goodness; even when we are tempted to waiver in what we know to be right. We want to generate greater self-discipline or self-control; even though we are tempted to monitor everybody else's business by imposing our power and limiting others' right to choose options that are "right" for them.

Of course, those with spiritual maturity understand that the Creator of the entire Universe, can and does answer the prayers of petitioners. Our spiritual journey in physical form is important for God. He is in partnership with each and every one of us. He can and does lift one out of depression and quells anxiety. He can and does reverse the course of a disabling or terminal illness. He can and does position people to obtain a job without any formal education or training to initially perform well in that job but their ultimate performance leaves no doubt that he or she was the right candidate for the job. He can and does align people for divine connections. God can and does provide us with our favorite pizza when we don't have two nickels to rub together. But to hold all of these material expectations as a determinant factor for us to have a relationship with God or for us to acknowledge the existence of God means that we don't know God.

Our spiritual maturity allows us to *"commit thyself to the way of the Lord"* even when we are not in receipt of God's material gifts. Those who have lost their way have not fully understood who and what God is. They cannot commit to the way of the Lord because they have difficulty discerning and differentiating their "needs" from their "wants." We need to have a full alignment with God during this spiritual journey within the physical form; yet, we typically want all the physical accoutrements of life. The Apostle Paul wrote to Titus, *"Our people must learn to devote themselves to doing what is good, in order to provide for urgent needs and not live unproductive lives."* (Titus, 3:24, NKJV) What is "good" is an attribute of God; therefore, a basic need that mature-minded spiritual sojourners pursue.

During our spiritual infancy, the lower level of our spiritual development, our "wants" eclipse our "needs." The child within us "wants what it wants when it wants it;" whereas, the adult within us "delays gratification for a future reward." Though our "wants" appear tantalizing, irresistible, and insatiable, our needs are still preeminent and if they were not, they wouldn't be needs. Abraham Maslow, a prominent psychologist, known for his theory that was published in his paper in 1943 entitled, "A Theory of Human Motivation," revealed a hierarchy of needs. He postulated that these needs are ascending and built upon one another from basic to aspirational needs. That is, the most basic human needs relate to food, clothing, and shelter or the basic physiological needs to ensure our survival. Ascending needs are only pursued after the previous needs are achieved.

The human organism, at any and all developmental levels, need nutritional sustenance, hydration, and oxygen to be able to exist at this very moment on this earthly plane with hope to progress to the next moment of existence. Institutions of higher learning, religious ritual engagements, and the pursuit of economic wellbeing are all foolish endeavors on its face when one cannot breathe. Who would care about worshiping God when there is no food or drink to nourish the body? Why would anyone consider obtaining a doctorate of philosophy degree when he or she has no hope of graduating from high school? There is no impetus in obtaining higher-order needs when basic level needs have not been achieved; nevertheless, once these physiological needs are obtained provides an opportunity to advance toward Maslow's second hierarchical need of safety.

Safety is critical for human evolution! We must feel safe in our communities, safe in our homes, and safe within our own skins if we are to advance beyond our animalistic impulses and through the self-preservation needs of ego (craving-heart realm) in order to enter the pure-heart realm. A common refrain in the Bible with God's first interactions with people was to "fear not." "Fear not," God tells Abraham (the father of Jewish, Christian and Islamic faiths). "Fear not," God tells Moses as he is instructed to return to Egypt to free the Jewish people from the tyranny of Pharaoh. "Fear not" is what Christ instructs of his own disciples throughout the New Testament. Fear erodes our sense of safety; thereby, stoking impotence. Fear triggers the primordial instinctual responses of fight, flight or freeze, and must be reined in if one is to advance to the next hierarchical need of belonging.

Humans are gregarious creatures or "herding animals." Our individual fragility is strengthened within our capacity to come together for mutual need and protection. Ostracizing from a community was often a death sentence; thus, safety was enhanced by our collectivism but this collectivism fosters the need for belonging and love. People in the 21st Century are starving for this sense of belonging and connection like never before. We must feel safe and secure if we are to risk belonging and connecting to others. Relating to our spiritual progression upon our spiritual journey, this desire for belonging/connection is a legitimate hunger need. Sure, there are hermits who choose isolation within the wilderness verse socialization within a community but those hermits are rare breeds; as Moses informs us in Genesis that it is not God's design that man exists alone. Even those considered deviating from the "normal" social groups, huddle together for identity, socialization, and survival. This need for fulfillment of belonging and connecting spurs us onto the next sequential need of enhancing self-esteem.

Our esteem needs are enhanced (or diminished) within self-introspection, conscious or subconscious mirroring, and interactions with others. We long for the enhancement of our self-esteem needs with validation, appreciation, praise, and accolades from others. The pursuit and attainment of knowledge ought to be sufficient as its own reward but the child doesn't run home exclaiming to his or her parent that great knowledge was obtained today; rather, the glory comes from the symbolic red letter "A" written by the teacher at the top of his or her test. Mom or Dad may have little interest in what the child has actually learned in school but burst at the seams with the prominently displayed, "A." Stars, stickers, grades, trophies, titles and other forms of public recognition enhance our prestige and reinforce the function of ego to distinguish and separate ourselves from others. When an enhanced self-esteem need is fulfilled it paves the way for Maslow's fifth and final hierarchical need—self-actualization.

I've often quipped that self-actualization is "realizing one's actual self." When each of the other preceding needs has been fulfilled this allows an opportunity to aspire toward our full potential. Creatively, emotionally, vocationally, intellectually, and spiritually, we are evolving to our greatest selves. The authenticity of the self is not hampered by perceptions and/or demands of others. Unencumbered by the pursuit of physiological, safety, belonging and esteem needs one has the ability to pursue esoteric needs as a capstone of our existence. Philosophically, we can pursue existential thoughts, metaphysics and greater scientific endeavors because we have successfully navigated through the preceding needs.

One may argue as to whether or not these human needs are hierarchical, developmental, sequential, essential, comprehensive, or exhaustive (as Maslow, himself, augmented the hierarchy of needs years later to include "transcendence;" thereby, including one's spiritual longings) but the notion behind the concept of "need" is that which is a "necessity" for our survival; whereas, "wants" encompasses "desires." Our wants are often hedonistic longings that do not often produce any substantive merit in one's life. Yes, there is a momentary pleasure with our hedonistic pursuits; otherwise, why would anyone pursue affairs, drugs or any antisocial behavior? I may "want" to dine at a New York City five-star restaurant to satisfy my taste buds and stoke the envy of others unable to afford to do so, but an enriched loaf of whole wheat bread and water may be all I "need" for daily survival. Christ was concerned about feeding our souls versus whetting our appetite for worldly pursuits. *"And Jesus said to them, 'I am the bread of life and he who comes to Me shall never hunger, and he who believes in Me shall never thirst.'"* (John 6:35; NKJV)

Maslow, with an afterthought, postulated the importance of spiritual transcendence but with forethought, I see the importance of spirituality as a central part of who we are. The recognition, pursuit, and fulfillment of our spiritual essence is why we've been gifted this journey; however, through our ignorance within this physical world, we grant credence over the physical part of ourselves and many negating our spiritual essence. This backward allegiance has us indulging our wants and neglecting our needs. Indeed, ego-centric beings (within the indifferent-heart and craving-heart realms) will always have their wants trump their needs. Spiritual maturity has sentient (and sapient) beings grasping for higher hanging spiritual fruit to satisfy their spiritual longings; whereas, the uninitiated gathers up whatever tangible byproducts of the material world that they see around them that fuels the fire of their unrelenting lust.

We need God, but within our ego-centric, animalistic, self-indulgent mindset the pursuit of our wants eclipses our need for God. We may need Maslow's first identified need of food, clothing and shelter but our want for hallucinogenic and amphetamine-like substances may leave us homeless, forego food and run nakedly down the street in a drug-induced haze. Likewise, safety (i.e. job security) may translate in fulfilling physiological needs (i.e., providing purchasing power for food, clothing, and shelter), but within our self-indulgence, we may opt to forego the job because we want to sleep in or play our video games. When we haven't captured what we are with the advancement of ourselves upon the spiritual continuum the need for God or the need for belonging, esteem, and self-actualization is trumped by the wants of the lower levels of our development. That is, the choice to belong at the lower levels of spiritual differentiation causes us to want to belong to deviant groups (e.g. gangs), engage in dysfunction, pursue disorder and experience distress.

When we earnestly reside in the pure-heart realm and recognize our "need" for God our "wants" for hedonistic pursuits diminish. Some religious adherents at the lower level of spiritual differentiation will insist that God is bestowing favor upon them and it clearly states so in the Bible. They will say that God will grant them the "desires of your heart;" therefore, we can hedonistically indulge in our "wants." This view is not sanctioned by God and we must read David's Psalm in full context. David wrote, *"Trust in the Lord, and do good; Dwell in the land, and feed on His faithfulness. Delight yourself also in the Lord, And He shall give you the desires of your heart. Commit your way to the Lord. Trust also in Him, And He shall bring it to pass."* (Psalm 37:3-5; NKJV)

The "wants" or "desires" of our hearts are contingent upon our relationship with God. The Pastor that informs us that God is in the business of granting us ten fingers adorn with gaudy, yet expensive rings; attire fresh off the runway of Paris and New York; along with automobiles that make neighbors green with envy is not a messenger of God. God is not trying to enhance our idolatry and lust. The pursuit of God is aligned with Godly ideals. God's promise; along with Abraham and Sarah's need for an heir, was not aligned with Sarah's plan to generate an offspring from her maidservant, Hagar. David, the boy who eventually became king and a man after God's own heart, desires, seduces, and impregnated another man's wife (Bathsheba), was not sanctioned by God. And, the Wisdom of Solomon affording him every human vanity (desire) including 700 wives and 300 concubines was not aligned with God's Wisdom; thus, Solomon deviated from a God-directed path to the worshiping of idols.

Trust in God is not about obtaining wish fulfillment and we can see this by God's refusal to remove the Apostle Paul's affliction. Paul wrote in his second letter to the church in Corinthians, *"Concerning this thing I pleaded with the Lord three times that it might depart from me. And He said to me, 'My grace is sufficient for you, for My strength is made perfect in weakness.'"* (2 Corinthians 12: 8-9; NKJV) Miracles are unconventional, unpredictable, and infrequent occurrences manifesting in a material world that God grants per His discretion and design; however, our lust for bobbles, fame, and wealth is not in line with God granting us the "desires of our hearts" that accompany the indifferent-heart and craving-heart realms. Purchasing a $29.99 prayer cloth will not grant you God's favor at the casino.

The spiritually adept are not pursuing their lusts (or hedonistic wants). Rather, our "need" for God changes our "desires" to be aligned with the Attributes of God. I desire peace. I don't want strife or contention with anyone or within myself. I desire the joy of the Lord and I attempt to choose happiness over despair on a daily basis. I desire faith; as I want it to vanquish my fears. I desire patience; thus, I try to be mindful that all I have is today and resist the temptation to rush toward tomorrow. I desire kindness, as I want to serve people along the way. I desire gentleness because I want my kindness to be tempered by civility. I desired goodness, in order to cogitate upon the appropriate standard of conduct. I desire discipline or self-control to comport myself based upon the standards that I proclaim to adhere to. Ultimately, I desire love to discern appropriate actions to bestow upon others and to expand this capacity to love even to my enemies.

The emphasis placed upon wants and needs seemingly shifts along with our degree of spiritual maturity on the spiritual differentiation continuum but in some ways that is an illusion. Our wants within the indifferent-heart realm appear to trump our needs and our needs seemingly trump our wants in the pure-heart realm but the truth is that each and every one of us will always do what we want and not always what it is that we need. Our wants are immature, ill-considered, and reactive while residing in the indifferent-heart realm because our ignorance is so profound. We just don't know that we don't know. In the opposite realm (pure-heart) our wants coincide with our needs to be more mature, thoughtfully considered, and deliberate with our actions. We are still "wanting" but our desires change significantly. Needs and wants are conflated in that I "need" God's Love but I also "want" God's Love. I am delighting more in the Lord and less in the accoutrements of a material world.

FEEDING THE SPIRIT

Fear is the domain of the material world. We have fear of failure, fear of success. We have fear of inadequacy and fear of not fitting in. We fear social rejection or the notoriety of a negative reputation. We fear losses and negative retributions from God. We feed on fear and fear metastasizes in our lives. Fear begins to feed on itself rendering us paralyzed to function well in life. God has never given us a "spirit of fear;" thus, the spiritual fruit we must cultivate to conquer fears is our faith. Faith vanquishes fear. Take this beginning step by analyzing areas of your fears with the following:

What fears are you running from?

- Intimacy
- Social interactions
- Success
- Tasks
- Performance

What things are you attacking based upon your fears?

- Self
- Minorities
- Religion
- Women
- Immigrants
- Indigent
- Political affiliation
- Ideologies
- Science
- God

How are you immobilized by your fears?

- Procrastination
- Slovenliness
- Torpor
- Failure
- Learned helplessness
- Substance Use/Abuse

NATURE RECLAIMS ITSELF

If you belonged to the world, it would love you as its own. As it is, you do not belong to the world, but I have chosen you out of the world. That is why the world hates you.
(John 15:19, NLT)

According to Psychology Today, anxiety impacts over 40 million people in America. The National Alliance for Mental Illness (NAMI) echoes these numbers and asserts that 17 million people have had an episode of major depressive disorder during the past year. One in 25 adults within America will experience mental illness within a given year, so what is going on with us in this world? Why are we tormented so much? It is one thing to be exiled from the garden due to disobedience of God but another thing to be exiled from God's Peace. Is this the unintended consequence of the gift that God has bestowed upon us? Is God holding on to His disappointment with humanity and extending His punishment to each of us due to the failures of Adam and Eve? Is He the vengeful God depicted in the Old Testament allowing His "waxed hot wrath" to torment our souls?

Our mental health is impacted by our biological inheritance; perhaps mom or dad, grandma or grandpa struggled with mental health issues and it has been genetically passed down to us. Or maybe it is our familial exposure in witnessing failed coping strategies within our family members that exasperates anxious/depressive symptoms. Perhaps the contributing factors are cultural, geographical, environmental, hormonal, or experientially based upon our present lived experiences and circumstances. Perhaps our mental distress is social; after all, who is not anxious about whether or not he or she will receive acceptance within a particular group? And, who is not experiencing depression when faced with feelings of disempowerment, rejection, or loss?

It is easy to worry about the future. We are apprehensive about things unknown. However, in the present, we worry about the vast amount of time we have ahead of us, the lack of time remaining, and what we should be doing in whatever time remains. We worry about the job we have or the job we don't have or the transition from one job to another. We worry about the strength of the relationship we have or the lack of a relationship if we don't have one or if we should end the relationship that we are in. We worry about the money we've saved or the fact that we haven't been able to save or the unexpected life circumstances that devastate our savings. We worry about the inevitability of our advanced age, the uncertain fragility of our health and our diminished mobility. The future taunts us with worries and concerns not yet evident that disrupt our peace of mind in the present, but remembering the past can help vanquish some of our fears of the future.

It is not true for everyone but many of us come from humble beginnings or disquieting pasts. Some of us have been hardened by what our pasts have produced; while others use the obstacles of their past as stepping stones to advance them along their life's journey. When I am ministering to people from a therapeutic setting, I remind people over and over again that worrying about anything is our failed and futile attempt to control the outcome of events. We ascribed to ourselves power that we just don't have when we endeavor to control the outcome of any event. I also let them know that whatever "insurmountable crisis" they have conjured up in their minds about an impending future are successful events they have conquered in the past. We do survive break-ups; many of them and go on to forge new relationships. We can survive failing grades or failing courses and go on to graduate from school. Few employers are concerned about an individual's performance within any particular class but the fact that we've persevered to graduation. We can survive job losses; as the termination from one job could be the "kick in our pants" we need to pursue a passion that we were initially afraid to pursue.

"If you belonged to the world, it would love you as its own…" Giving credence to the world keeps us in fear. Now, this is not to say that human beings don't have agency. We do! Not only are we made in the image of God; who is Omnipresent, Omnipotent, Omniscient and Omnibenevolent, God grants us dominion over this earthly plane. Recorded in Moses' first book, Genesis, is his account of God's Directive for humans to *"[b]e fruitful and multiply; fill the earth and subdue it; have dominion over the fish of the sea, over the birds of the air, and over every living thing that moves on the earth"* (Genesis, 1:28, NKJV). Thus, humans are at the apex of God's creation (and why wouldn't we be as "children" of God)? Nevertheless, as powerful as we are, God doesn't grant us power over the future, nor must we be constrained by the narratives of our past.

Soothsayers, clairvoyants, and prognosticators claim to have a clear vision of the future but in God's Omniscient Wisdom, He has withheld a clear vision of our future from us. Of course, the Creator of the Universe transcends all time. He told Jeremiah, *"Before I formed you in the womb, I knew you,"* and we are made in the image of God, but we are not in parity with God. If the future was made clear for each and every one of us, there would be no mystery ahead of us, little need for God, and certainly no need for faith in God. Indeed, there would be little value in the gift of our presence upon this earth if every conceivable experience has been preconceived. Our ego may manifest greatly and our faith may diminish entirely; thus, that which is "created" would believe itself to be as powerful or more powerful than the Creator.

Our presence impacts the world but the world also impacts us tremendously! A truism about the world is that nature reclaims itself. I have witnessed longstanding and thriving businesses demise or come to an abrupt end with a shifting economy. I've witnessed some of those same businesses abandon their stores with blight moving in and nature starts reclaiming the building. Parking lots, once pristine and paved, sprouts vegetation breaking through the cracks it produces, covers the lot, and climbs the building. Indeed, we humans are derived from dust and return to dust after a short stint upon the planet. And, as a therapist who sees the unyielding recycling of those with mental illness, return again and again with the same life stressors reveals our human nature in reclaiming our wounded selves.

Whether biological, environmental, or psychological beings, in nature we are reclaiming our mental illness like the once paved parking lot sprouting with weeds. As spiritual beings, we do not belong to the world but our vision of who we are is skewed. We are tormented by the world because we grant allegiance to the world. Christ assures us in the opening scripture that He has chosen us out of the world because the world, though necessary for our physical experience, is not the essence of who we are upon this spiritual journey. He goes further to say, *"...In the world you will have tribulation; but be of good cheer, I have overcome the world"* (John 16:33, NKJV). Jesus, the representative of the Most High God, exemplifies for us a *way* for mental stability with the revelation of *truth* to experience *life*.

The "way" is not Christianity, Judaism, or Islamic. The "way" is not Hinduism, Buddhism, or Confucianism. The "way" is not religious, political or economic *["...render to Caesar the things that are Caesar's..."* (Mark 12:17; NKJV)]. The "way" is not medical, pharmaceutical, or psychological. The "way" (as exemplified by Jesus) is the direction of our spirit as we return home to God; because in the realm of spirit, God reclaims Himself by redeeming His children. God doesn't endorse, plague or inflict mental illness upon us. It is not God's desire or design that we are mentally disturbed. Indeed, Jesus reminds us, *"Peace I leave with you, My peace I give to you; not as the world gives do I give to you. Let not your heart be troubled, neither let it be afraid"* (John 14:27, NKJV).

The world is a creation of God but our relationship to the world is socially constructed. Our level of spiritual differentiation determines the meaning of our experience within the material world. Though the Diagnostic and Statistical Manual of Mental Disorders, Fifth Edition (DSM-5) distinguishes fears (imminent perceived or real threat) from anxiety (anticipation of future threat), I have asserted that anxiety is the manifestation of our fears. After all, we are not "anxious" around the dog if we weren't "fearful" of being bitten. Our apprehensiveness about the future generates worries. Worriers attempt to control the outcome of events. The language we (therapists) used for "anxiety" previously was "neurosis" until the word (label) became stigmatizing; however, those with "neuroticism" or "anxiety" overly focus upon themselves. They are over-thinkers, feel overly responsible, and over-reactive to a contrived set of circumstances. They give themselves over to the world, snatching the control from God and try to manage life themselves.

Anxiety goes hand in hand with each overarching mental health disorder (i.e., anxiety disorders, mood disorders, psychotic disorders). A collapsed, deflated or fragmented ego state lacks ego integrity and operates out of the limitations of itself versus tapping into the Abundance of God. This neurotic, self-focused pathology, called, "anxiety" dovetails with depression. Depressed people are besieged with negative attributions of self, others and their futures. A fully functioning, intact ego-state implodes, or collapses to impede our ability to function. Depressed people entertain faulty notions of themselves. If not voiced out loud the internal dialogue will be, "I'm no good" (negative attribute of self), "nobody likes me" (negative attributes of others), and "everything I do will fail" (negative attributions toward future). These negative perceptions all stem from a "neurotic" (anxious) view of ourselves.

From a psychological perspective, psychosis (indeed, all mental health disorders) is a complex and complicated disorder with multiple theories of causation, with various treatment modalities (largely pharmaceutical) with often chronic mental health interventions and dubious prognosis. The etiology of psychosis could be the genetic legacy inherited from previously afflicted family members, brain injury or trauma, substance-induced (from marijuana to methamphetamines), an aging brain, or environmental conditions. There is a high comorbid occurrence of psychosis and anxiety and when I am working with clients with psychosis, I focus on the anxiety. Anxiety can trigger one's psychosis and of course, experiencing psychosis is often anxiety-producing.

To restate the above, anxiety is a manifestation of our fears, depression is negative alterations in mood or cognition and psychosis is a split from reality. All of which, stem from a disturbed mind and from a spiritual perspective, all stem from alienation from (or distorted view of) God and disfellowship from one another in our human family. Since "nature reclaims itself" and fear is a byproduct of having a human experience in this physical world, mental illness will also be a byproduct of our human experience. Nevertheless, we are "spiritual beings" having a "human experience" thus, we are assured that, *"For God has not given us a spirit of fear, but of power and of love and of a sound mind"* (2 Timothy 1:7, NKJV). The love of God is paramount but the love from our fellow human beings is also significant and critical. God's Love gets meted out within our human interactions and if dispensed appropriately, many of us would be free of mental health concerns.

Let's look at the emotional reactivity of a fragmented ego state that chooses a suicide option resulting from a lost love. It has been my experience that males/females, blacks/whites, young/old, pagan or Christian individuals struggle mightily with the prospect of a lost love. A young, black, Christian lady or an older, white, pagan guy would have a greater capacity to deal with a lost love versus having an emotional collapse resulting in a suicide attempt if either understood that rejection of a relationship is not a rejection of him or her. Psychologist Erick Erickson postulated in his eight stages of psychosocial development the first critical stage is forging trust vs. mistrust. We need to know that our physical and intimate world is safe, secure, and dependable. We may intuitively know and trust in the spiritual essence of a loving God prior to transitioning into the material world but our focus quickly changes with our dependency, safety, and security placed in the hands of primary care providers.

These care providers, and many of them are extraordinary exemplars of God's Love, succeed in shaping the positive vision we have of ourselves. After all, one in twenty-five Americans impacted by mental illness per year are only four percent of the American population. Our very presence is a gift of goodness bestowed upon us by a Loving God. Our loving care providers replicate the safe, secure and trusting environment that they, too, have encountered prior to the transition from the spiritual realm to the physical world. As children of the Most-High God, we each possess a core of goodness. We know that God is Good and we are told that *"[h] e who does good is of God, but he who does evil has not seen God*" (3 John 1:11, NKJV). Those who know God, truly know God, are aware of God's unmerited favor bestowed upon them and readily exemplify this goodness in service to others.

Unfortunately, not everyone enters this world into a trusting environment. Some, right after birth, may have insecure attachments. They may have neglectful or abusive care providers. Some have been victimized in utero. Whether our initial attachments were secure or insecure the world feeds our fears. It is a natural by-product of living in a transient, impermanent and uncertain world. Our anxiety is intense because we are in a state of perpetual fear. The world is scary and if nature truly does reclaim itself, then the world perpetuates and reclaims its fears. Nevertheless, the good news is that we are spiritual beings having a human experience. As a result, we're told and assured that we are "*in the world but not of the world.*" This bodes well for the spiritual-minded, but those seeking psychological relief can practice the exercises within Edmund Bourne's, "The Anxiety and Phobia Workbook." Bourne asserts that the remedy for anxiety is to reduce physiological reactivity, eliminate avoidance behaviors and change subjective interpretations (self-talk).

What is the "physiological reactivity" associated with anxiety? My clients have experienced trembling, hot flashes, cold flashes, profuse sweating, choking sensations, heart palpitations, and panic so severe that they feel as though they are dying. Some experience somatization, paralysis, or enhanced sensitivity to chronic pain. One client expressed to me that his anxiety was so palpable that he would lose mobility and functioning in his legs, collapsing as he made his way from one room to another. Some have experienced uncontrollable crying jags; whereas, others felt momentarily asthmatic episodes, with an inability to catch a breath.

These physiological responses resulting from anxiety are very distressing; thus, we tend to avoid situations, circumstances, and individuals that we believe might trigger such physiological responses. People may avoid attending sporting events due to the size of crowds or the grocery store due to the faulty perception of being judged. We may forgo educational pursuits or have a substantially limited educational experience due to fears of not fitting in, alienation, or ostracism. Others find limited longevity on the job due to palpable fear that correction is criticism; thus, criticism is perceived as rejection. They will abandon the job in short order versus enduring a perceived blow to their fragile psyches. Dr. Tara Brach, in her article called, "Radical Compassion in Challenging Times" states the worrying and fears "interfere with our executive functioning, making good decisions." And, further, she writes, "They interfere with our capacity to feel compassion for others…" and our ability "…to move wisely on our path."

When we are in the world, gossip, social media, and our reputation may be assailed by others but it is really what we believe and say about ourselves that has a huge impact upon us. We, too, whisper faulty notions "into our own ears" that grossly distort (within our own minds) the image that God has of us. Our negative self-talk fuels the negative perception of our fragile psyches and gives credence to our fears and avoidant behaviors. It is a perpetual cycle that feeds upon itself, allowing this "fear monster" to grow enormously and paralyzing performance. Fear is a human construction and an archetype of our existence with the material world. Fear is a primordial human emotion, perhaps a legitimate warning signal alerting us to the dangers within the material world but fear is the antithesis of God.

God is a spiritual entity…a spiritual being. Nothing that is material can produce spirit. Nature may reclaim itself and indeed may have its own energy but it cannot produce spirit. A rock, within nature, may have substance, form, utility, and even latent energy but it lacks the sentience and/or awareness of spirit. The rock doesn't know it is a rock and the tree doesn't know that it is a tree. If we fashion the tree into a table the tree doesn't know it was transformed into a table and nor does the table know that it comes from the tree. God is not material but God (The Creator) can create the sensation of a material world. Consider, when we dream, there is substance, form, sensation, emotions, interpersonal connectedness, wistful past re-creations, and superhuman fantasies. Our dream life can lustfully link us to an adored celebrity crush, allow us to scuba dive the clear blue waters in the Caribbean or rocket us to outer galaxies with wings made of gold.

Our dream life is absent of time. It has no sequential order or logic. Our dream life can transport us back to childhood, reliving the taunting from an unforgettable bully. Though my adult son and I have been on road trips together within his adulthood, the typical dreams that I have when he's featured in the dream, he is a child. I do take some cursory stabs at psychoanalyzing myself as to why he is mainly a child in my dreams but then push my dream analysis aside due to having a vivid and rich dream life. I have had some prophetic dreams that have come true and some repetitive dreams or some unforgettable "prophetic" dreams that have never come true. I have had the typical anxiety dreams where I am lost and can't find my way back home or have parked someplace and can't find my car. I have had bizarre dreams that have no rhyme or reason and sad dreams where I wake up in tears (which are odd for me in that most things in my waking life do not reduce me to tears). Whatever "materializes" in a dream state has no enduring presence outside of the dream; thus, God's Consciousness can create form, substance, and the material essence of our experiences (i.e. the rock) but nature cannot create God.

When the Pharisees attempted to trick Christ Jesus with their question about taxes, Christ replied, *"Render therefore to Caesar the things that are Caesar's, and to God's the things that are God's,"* (Matthew, 22:21, NKJV). In like fashion, we render to nature, the world, and the things of this world to be reclaimed by nature. And, we, sentient beings and children of the Most-High God return to God. God redeems all souls and whatever pieces of ourselves that were a part of our nature are stripped away and the purity of spirit returns home to God.

FEEDING THE SPIRIT

Nature will ultimately reclaim our physical bodies. Whatever we loved or hated about our physical bodies will join all things in nature, to experience entropy and return to the earth from which it came. Our enduring essence is our spirit, however, just like our physical essence, "we are what we eat," the quality of our spiritual existence in this world is contingent upon what we place into our spirit. Recall what God told Moses, "...I AM WHO I AM..." (Exodus 3:14, NKJV). "I am" is a declarative statement in the present tense about who we are. It is not a declaration of the past or projecting a future but a statement of our core beliefs at this very moment. "I am worthless" or "I am a failure" are declarative statements but they are not of God. "I am courageous...I am fearless...I am powerful," etc. are statements representative of God. Reciting these types of affirmations on a daily basis will change the vision of who we are.

WHATEVER GOD IS, WE ARE!

Follow only what is good. Remember that those who do good prove that they are God's children, and those who do evil prove that they do not know God.
(3 John 1:11; NLT)

Whatever we believe God is, we are. The Apostle Paul cites in his epistle to the Galatians some of the attributes of God, known as the "Fruit of the Spirit." Of course, God is comprised of many things…indeed everything, but these fruit of the spirit are important attributes that represent God. Not everyone will conclude that God actually exists and for those who grant incredulity to a living, omniscient, omnipotent, omnipresent, and omnibenevolent God may not grant God the affirming attributes represented in the list of nine fruit of the spirit enumerated by Paul. As a therapist, it may be beyond my purview and ability to instill within others that a living, loving, and involved God exists for those deeply rooted within opposing positions; nevertheless, if God is love, we aspire to love.

Love is the essence of our existence. It is hardwired into our "spiritual DNA." It is a legitimate hunger need that satiates the psyche and soul. It is an invisible substance working like "relational glue" bonding together families, neighborhoods, and humanity throughout the world. Replicated in God's Love for us is our love for one another. It is heartwarming and awe-inspiring to see this love pouring out of children, adolescents, adults, community organizations, religious communities of all faiths, and nation-states all over the world. Love is courageous; thus, a mother will fight off a bear and a father will jump into a lion pit to protect his child (and in many times to protect a stranger's child). Love is transformative and I've seen some people of hate transform their lives due to the power of love.

Love obliterates artificial demarcations that separate one person from another. A child, not fully inculcated with "stranger-danger fears," walks up to and engages a smelly, old, tattered clothed, homeless man in conversation like they were long-lost friends. Young children will braid beaded bracelets, sell lemonade or go door-to-door collect funds in service to others. Adolescents shaped by a despicable tragedy within their school, rise up to forge a national sociopolitical movement to produce change. Adults, following a hurricane or natural disaster, leave the comforts of their families, jobs, and communities to venture forward, residing in readymade shelters, to serve people they don't even know. Organizations and business leaders abandon their profit-making specialties to make much-needed respirators in a global pandemic. Faith-based religious communities rally their members for school supplies or meals and medicine to meet the demand of people who are in need. This is love exemplified!

If God is love, we are nourished by love, sustained by love and replicate this love to others in the world. And, to the humanist that decries, "It is just human decency, reaffirming the basic core of human goodness being manifested," I say that love remains an attribute of God even if God's Essence is denied. There is no reason for the existence of sentient beings if there is no God and there is no reason for love if there are no sentient beings. And for the empirical atheist that can't abide in an entity that is imperceptible to the sense receptors, what about an intangible mind, black holes, or notions of other dimensions? With awareness, we have the ability to choose (not simply to react) and with choice, we can choose the concept of love over lust. Should we choose lust, we make an idol of God in the form of money, fame, power, etc. and then we pursue those idols at the expense of our spiritual evolution.

God is peace? God "embodies" peace and lets us know that He wishes to grant us equipoise. Christ informs us in Matthew 11:28 (NKJV) to *"Come to Me, all you who labor and are heavy laden, and I will give you rest."* And further, *"Be of good comfort, be of one mind, live in peace; and the God of love and peace will be with you"* [II Corinthians 13:11 (NKJV)]. It is not of God's purpose or plans that we are mentally, emotionally, or spiritually disturbed. I've met many clients seeking psychotherapy, pharmaceutical intervention, or even illegal substance use/abuse as a means to find peace. Many of those, even those expressing a belief in God, have deviated from their spiritual trajectory toward God and lost their peace. Peace is not a place or destination; it is a state of mind. Jesus stated, *"My peace I leave with you…"* (John 14:27, NKJV). Jesus' peace is His example of how we should live a life undisturbed (that takes practice).

When we erect idols of agitation, fear, doubt, or worries, it robs us of our peace. We give credence to a false deity that will incessantly disturb our peace. Many, including myself at times, grant credence to a material world; along with fleeting emotions, thereby, succumbing to the very thing we believe. We denounce God's peace and prostrate ourselves to these idols of deception. The Israelites bore witness to the majesty of God but repeatedly succumbed to their own fears and doubts. And, before we take a haughty and dismissive look at them, remember that we too have often cowered in the face of uncertainties and turned our allegiance away from God. We, too, allow ourselves to be seduced by the world and forget that we are spiritual beings of higher order. Even with my spiritual awareness, I must sustain daily practice to choose faith over fears.

That is, a young man may bemoan the fact that he is anxious all of the time and lacks motivation. He bows down to the idol of daily cannabis use and will exclaim, "I want a different outcome in my life but you can't take my marijuana away from me!" He'll refute any characterization of it as a "drug," rationalizes all the recent states that are legalizing this drug and rejects any notion that he may be suffering from cannabis-induced anxiety that also robs him of his motivation to succeed. Likewise, another client will present in therapy, who finds that her marriage is crumbling beneath her but she refuses to release the hedonistic idol, represented in her ongoing lust for her paramour in order to save her marriage. One cannot find peace if we refuse to cultivate peace.

I have found that to be in receipt of these spiritual attributes from God that I must go to God daily and request to be nourished by the fruit that He has so generously laid out for us to consume. I cannot be adequately nourished on sustenance I consumed a year ago…a month ago, or a day ago. These "spiritual nutrients" fuels the "spiritual body" in order to develop "spiritual muscles" to engage within "spiritual practice." Oh, I can be lackadaisical or lazy in my pursuit of godly attributes at times, and my "spiritual muscles" atrophy when I am not working out with God. However, I do recognize my imperfections and try not to beat myself up for them. I simply remain steadfast in my journey ahead and let go of the idols (and "weeds" additionally, as idols attract us and weeds choke us off from spiritual production) that I am erecting and return to building my faith in God who has already granted me peace (*"Now the God of Peace be with you all."* Romans 15:33; NKJV). While at peace, we can focus on what is good.

If God is good (*"Why do you call Me good? No one is good but One, that is, God"* Luke 18:19 NKJV), then our duties and responsibilities are to mimic the standards that God has exemplified as we are marching through this world. Whether it is fulfilling the instructions within a recipe book to replicate some meal we might like, or to responsibly perform the duties of one's profession, we must adhere to standards. It is (sometimes) tragically amusing but often dismaying to see clients trying to receive a desired outcome but to reject the standards that are in place for the desired outcome to occur. We abdicate standards for expediency and the cost can be devastating. Our overarching value is love but it is fascinating to see how quickly we sacrifice our standards for love when we fear loneliness. I don't assert that people have to adopt the standards of others but they are violating the standards that they claim to have.

We are called upon as therapists, or ministers, or laypeople in general, to come to the aid of those who genuinely wants our assistance in redirecting their paths back to God. Those fixated upon idolatry will not want our wise counsel. They seek an audience to extol narratives of their victim's status but we are not going to be able to make sense out of their nonsense. We cannot impose our standards upon another person; even to keep them safe. It has been my experience that no matter what therapeutic intervention I pull from my "bag of therapeutic tricks," clients always do what they want to do. Their intransigence lasts for years and clients go from therapist to therapist singing the same old sad song with little or no change in trajectory. God lays out standards of conduct for all of us but it only appeals to those who have already chosen to honor a spiritual path.

Idolatry is submission to a false god. One could argue that the architect or designer of these false gods that tempt us away from the Ultimate God is the devil but I am disinclined to disavow our personal responsibility in this journey in life by attributing our poor choices to a malevolent force outside of ourselves. Indeed, anything we worship and grant our allegiance to is our idol...our god. The false notions we attribute to God become our god and we serve it. The drug addict prays for his/her next fix, yields to the sovereignty of that drug in his/her life, and witnesses to others about the pseudo appeal of the drug. Heroin addicts rave about heroin, with their nose turned up towards those using meth. There is elitism within cocaine users over those using "crack." Cannabis users deny that marijuana is even a drug, but whatever the idol, people's devotion to their idol is clear.

If God is wrathful, punitive, jealous, abandoning, rejecting, or non-existing; so are we. Some Bible clutching Christians have embraced the person and policies of an evil president, along with his cronies that I'm sure Christ would have labeled a "brood of vipers." If God segregates people into camps of those who are acceptable to him and those who are unacceptable, we too justify notions of inclusion and exclusion. If God doesn't exist for the atheist, then there is no belief in the continuation of spirit or a belief that we are spirit. Our spirit determines the direction that we will go in life. The spiritual orientation that we have in the world that is absent of the knowledge of God endorses worldly pursuits. The hunger for anything other than the Attributes of God will leave us malnourished and incessantly wanting. Author Osborn, in "The Axis and the Rim" echoes these sentiments with, "Human beings suffer from a deep sense of incompleteness, which expresses itself in continuous craving."

If God is rigid in His thinking and intolerant of diverse views, it makes sense to adopt our own fundamental views and impose our narrow values upon others. Jon Meacham tackles this issue in his book, "The Hope of Glory: Reflections on the Last Words of Jesus from the Cross." Meacham wrote, "Literalism is for the weak; fundamentalism is for the insecure. Both are sins, too, against God, for to come to believe that we are in an exclusive possession of the truth about things beyond time and space, and thus hold the power to shape lives and decisions about things within time and space, is to put ourselves in the place of God." Well said, Meacham, as literalism and fundamentalism is the hallmark of the indifferent-heart realm but we also must be careful about the rationalism and critical (cynical) analysis that resides in the craving-heart realm.

If God is kindness and gentleness that is equated with the fruit of the spirit then our responsibility is to administer service and civility to the people we encounter. Many may see kindness and gentleness as synonyms but the Apostle Paul wouldn't have had proclaimed the nine distinctive "Fruit of the Spirit" within his epistle to the Galatians if there wasn't a distinction between the two. "Kindness" is a benign action, whether in word choice or behavior that is bestowed upon self and others. It is a call to action to serve in the way of Christ; an exemplar of service. It is notable that even after His resurrection, Christ is still in service mode and prepares breakfast for the disciples (John 21). "Gentleness" is conveyed within the tone, attitude, and spirit in which the kind action is bestowed. Who really wants the gift of kindness if it is begrudgingly given?

As a therapist, I am obliged by my profession, state licensure, and by an implicit agency mandate to be kind to those presenting for therapy. My service flows through acquired knowledge and skill but gentleness is the attitude that I bring to this professional engagement. As a spiritual sojourner, I am obliged by spiritual values and principles to be a representative of kindness that exemplifies God. In doling out this spiritual fruit of kindness it can spoil easily if not accompanied by "gentleness." What real benefit is it to be in receipt of, or to dispense to others, the fruit of kindness with a begrudging spirit? I don't want someone showing up to help me with health issues, chores, or moving into a new residence who complains vociferously throughout the experience. I don't want to be the one to show up at a wedding ceremony or church sermon and expressing my dissatisfaction to all of those who choose to hear. There truly is value bestowed upon people through the act of kindness but the value loses resonance when kindness is not tempered by gentleness.

If God is joy then in a sporadically appearing bleak, dark, and miserable world, we must seek joy. James, the half-brother of Jesus, instructs us, *"My brethren, count it all as joy when you fall into various trials…"* (James, 1:2, NKJV). And, in Psalms, we learn, *"But let all those rejoice who put their trust in You; Let them ever shout for joy, because You defend them; Let those also who love Your name be joyful in You."* (Psalms 5:11, NKJV) God wants our life experience to be joyful. He has no vested interest in us experiencing pain. God derives no perverse pleasure when we experience torment and agony. So, "Why God, why does our future appear bleak, darkness prevails and suffering continues?" This is a question of the ages and certainly a question that many of my stricken clients might ask.

I recall seeing a television interview of a beautiful one-legged, ex-military, a roadside bomb injured, para-Olympian expressing that she has done more with her life since losing her leg than she would have ever imagined and have done prior to losing her leg. Her loss prompted her to live, having had a personal encounter with death. The loss of her leg was tragic but joy radiated from her in the interview despite her loss. God doesn't guarantee our lives with a particular outcome but He does ensure us, given that He is Joy, we can have joy despite our circumstances. If our world is bleak, dark, and miserable, our vision has been skewed by the narrow focus upon ourselves versus focusing upon the expansiveness of a Universal God. Joy can occur with the mindfulness of the moment. Joy is etched in the face of a crinkled smile from an elderly person who reaches out with a feeble hand of thanks for your mere presence of sitting with her. Joy comes in the aroma of freshly brewed coffee in the mornings. Joy comes when we purposely slow down with patient appreciation of each moment.

If God is Patience and we venerate God, we learn to "wait on God." We learn to not be reactive to urgencies and to discern appropriate choices that lead to positive outcomes. In a therapeutic setting, I have seen the cost of haste in the lives of clients. I have listened to the agony of regret with those who walked off the job simply because they didn't like the corrective feedback from a supervisor. I've listened with amazement and frustrated by the clients' resistance to wise counsel by moving a person into their homes that they've met only 24 hours previously. I am waving the red flags of danger…danger…danger in the face of the clients who summarily dismiss my warnings only to return a short time later regretting having not heeded my warnings. Of course, when reviewing the clients' records I can see the repetitive history of those ignoring the lessons of patience, lunging full speed ahead into predictable dilemmas with catastrophic outcomes.

Patience involves a degree of tolerance. We'll encounter people with views and opinions that are totally alienated from our ideas and positions but we must have patience to not view the person through a skewed lens that lessens their spiritual essence in our eyes. When we lowered the estimation of people, we cease to be tolerant and can bring harm. We never harm anyone that we respect as equal. The moment we denigrate a person in our thoughts, we deride them with our language and reflect this negative notion in our behaviors. Throughout the bible, we have seen God tolerate our ineptitude. God demonstrates His patience in His empathy, understanding, and forgiveness. Remember that Christ told Peter that he is to forgive people seventy times seven. This will require a whole lot of patience! Our patience allows us to cope with the fallibility of humans (including ourselves), while placing our faith in God.

If God is faithful, then we can trust in our relationship with God. We can patiently wait on God because God got our backs. We don't have to have loneliness or fears govern our mate selection choices. Rather, we can have faith, if governed by Godly standards, that God will bring into our lives the ideal mate to meet our needs at our level of spiritual differentiation. We don't have to feed the weed of doubt because God is bigger than our doubts. *"But let him ask in faith with no doubting, for he who doubts is like a wave of the sea driven and tossed by the wind"* (James 1:6; NKJV). God's faithful example can now be meted out in our relationships with others. It is hard to commit to principles we adhere to when the seduction of the world constantly tempts us but we must continuously hone our faith or we'll easily fall.

Conversely, if God is chaos, then the world is chaos! It is a random universe with random events, random occurrences, and random outcomes. Scientific methods attempt to do away with the randomness of events by projecting order into the "chaos" to have determined outcomes, but science is provisional. Nevertheless, "hats off" to science as humanity are the beneficiaries of great scientific achievements. The misconception of science is that it is at odds with a faith-based understanding of God; however, it is God's discipline in creating order out of a disordered, chaotic universe that brings about our human construction of science. Iyanla Vanzant counters chaos with love and writes in her book, "Forgiveness" with, "Even in the midst of total chaos, pain, and dysfunction, love is calling us to a higher experience and expression."

The world pandemic of the Coronavirus (COVID-19) is frightening and economically disabling with future uncertainties but a Loving God is not in the pandemic. The racism and inhumanity exhibited by Derek Chauvin toward George Floyd are not of God. Global warming that is developing hurricanes with greater intensity and frequency are decimating communities, but that is not of God. God is not chaotic. Just because these earth challenging events are upon us does not mean that God doesn't remain in control. God is omniscient, orderly, and strategic, as well as existing beyond time; thus, He has the patience to allow for the unfolding of seemingly random events to fit within His Grand Old Design. Chaos is leveled out through God's spiritual attribute of discipline/self-control. Resulting from this Godly attribute (discipline/self-control), order flowed from the void and then the seemingly chaotic universe to culminate into our very presence at this moment and time. I have no idea what will come from this incredible chaos of 2020 but God remains in control. The God of Love is the God of Goodness; thus, evil will be pushed back and God will prevail.

Given that God is Self-Controlled and/or Disciplined, it becomes one of the fruit produced and passed on to each and every one of us. We mimic this fruit in the effort we employ on a daily basis. As a doctorate degree therapist, I have embarked upon the discipline of social work and psychology in order to engage within my profession. Further, this (and all disciplines) takes practice. The writings I generate take discipline and practice. Diligently, I string together a slew of words that I hope has coherence, meaning, and value; no matter how imperfectly done. Though God is perfect, the Fruit of the Spirit offered up to us is "goodness." We discipline ourselves and practice to achieve this standard of goodness versus an unattainable goal of perfection from imperfect beings. We are more than our professions; thus, spiritual beings need "self-control or discipline" to practice the spiritual attributes listed by the Apostle Paul.

God's existence is not contingent upon what we believe but our notion of "gods/idols" (the "things" that we submit to) is manifested in whatever it is that we believe. The pursuit of mammon is the antithesis of God but God grants us the freedom to pursue whatever life experience we wish to have upon this earthly plane. The god of an atheist is oneself. The god of an agnostic is confusion. The god of humanism is rationalism. The god of hedonism is wanton lust. The god of nature is animism. The god of socio-ethnic stratification is racism. The god of gender dominance/suppression is sexism. And, the god of mammon is capitalism. As we struggle to determine where we place our allegiance, I'll end this chapter with how I started it, *"Follow only what is good. Remember that those who do good prove that they are God's children, and those who do evil prove that they do not know God."* (3 John 1:11; NLT)

FEEDING THE SPIRIT

God's attributes are innumerable! If we were to attempt to mimic and perfect the inexhaustible attributes of God, it would stop us in our tracks and likely send us back to darkness where little effort is needed to engage within hedonism. However, the Apostle Paul generated a list of nine spiritual attributes that we can focus upon and hone our spirituality. Use the list below to chart where you are at on a daily basis and use your honest rating to propel you in the direction you choose to go.

Detached	2	3	4	5	6	7	8	9	10	Love/Praxis
Stress/worry	2	3	4	5	6	7	8	9	10	Peace
Sad/depressed	2	3	4	5	6	7	8	9	10	Joy
Doubt/fear	2	3	4	5	6	7	8	9	10	Faith
Inconsiderate	2	3	4	5	6	7	8	9	10	Kindness
Harsh/mean	2	3	4	5	6	7	8	9	10	Gentleness
Angry/hurried	2	3	4	5	6	7	8	9	10	Patience
Slovenly	2	3	4	5	6	7	8	9	10	Discipline
Evil/backward	2	3	4	5	6	7	8	9	10	Goodness

CHARACTER VS. REPUTATION

We can rejoice, too, when we run into problems and trials, for we know that they help us develop endurance. And endurance develops strength of character, and character strengthens our confident hope of salvation.
(Romans 5:3-4, NLT)

In the twenty-one centuries following the death of Christ and how the Western world marks historical time, along with the twenty plus centuries preceding Christ's birth, humanity has been defined by its reputation. The Internet, replete with the enormity of social media sites, can spread the reputation of individuals, organizations, and governments throughout the world like wildfire. I don't think that I've fully appreciated the impact of one's reputation in the lives of individuals until I started working as a therapist in a rural, SW Minnesota community. Anonymity is virtually nonexistent, with innuendoes, gossip, and characterizations made about people simply in the passing. It is no wonder why clients have been mortified going into the local HyVee or Walmart with an accurate perception that others are judging them. That is, each of us scan, assess, and make some type of judgment (label) about the person we see (e.g. safe, frightening, weird, jerk, attractive, etc.).

Some clients have been emotionally paralyzed by social media posts from family, friends, and anonymous sources, which they feel has sullied their reputation and attacked their character. Others present with emotional volatility. They vehemently voice their outrage in a therapy session, vowing their intention for retaliation in like-minded fashion or more severely for those who have assailed their reputation. More broadly speaking, we can see the emotionally paralyzing fear in the impotence exhibited in the Republican Party by those fearful of a wayward tweet. At one point, I had had great respect for the reputation of the Republican Party but during the Trump regime, I have been shocked to see their lack of character. In many ways, people have concluded that one's reputation and character are one and the same. We do ourselves a terrible disservice when we conflate the two.

Clients develop social phobias, generalized anxiety, and avoidance tendencies that intern them within a self-constructed prison; thereby, avoiding interactions with others they perceive will judge them by their reputation. Oftentimes, there isn't a definitive indictment lodged upon the individual's character but an unfounded fear that others are judging them harshly. Nevertheless, character is not in the hands of others. Character is often revealed by the consistency of one's behaviors over a span of time. That is, our "character" becomes the creation of our own making; whereas, our "reputation" becomes what other people decide. There is a non-exhaustive list of attributes, both positive and negative, that can reveal the nature of one's character. Positive character traits can be loyal, forthright, benevolent, studious, trustworthy, dependable, hardworking, determined, goal-oriented, tenacious, patient, faithful, lovable, kind, etc.

Of course, we can adopt some negative character traits that can also define us like being stubborn, hardhearted, lazy, dishonest, reckless, irresponsible, treacherous, hateful, wrathful, exploitive, manipulative, and the like. We have the capacity to shape and refine our character. We can establish our core beliefs and decide how we'll manifest those beliefs to the world. The world then makes its own assessment of our character traits which becomes a subjective determination about our reputations. If we have worked diligently upon our character, we'd hope that it would be reflected in the minds of others in terms of our reputation; however, throughout history and within our own lives, character doesn't always align with reputation and reputation is not necessarily a true representation of our character.

Think about the Biblical hero of the boy named, David and the king named, Saul. It wasn't a part of God's design that the twelve tribes of Israel would have a king in command; however, God relented to the wishes of the people and allowed them to create a monarchy with Samuel's (prophet of God) anointing. Saul was anointed as the sovereign king of the people of Israel. Saul was anointed, consecrated, set apart by God, Himself, to be the first king of Israel; therefore, what better reputation does anyone need? Saul had a good reputation as a warrior and commander, and later the first anointed king of Israel but his character waned as David's character and reputation began to eclipse Saul's reputation. Saul reacted to the "social media" of his time with the women singing, *"Saul has slain his thousands, and David his ten thousands"* (I Samuel 18:7; NKJV).

It is interesting; yet, sad to see how quickly one's character is sacrificed for the sake of one's reputation. David was a shepherd boy, also anointed by the prophet Samuel to become the next king. Of course, this was no big deal for the accomplished King Saul with his plate full in dealing with the pending war with the Philistines. The combatants were on the battlefield, poised for war, with the Israeli's forgetting about their previous victories while aligning themselves with God. Weak-kneed they gasped at the sight of Goliath, the Philistine's fiercest warrior. The Philistine's implored the Israelis to send forth their finest warrior and they could do battle, one on one, without subjecting either side to a slaughtering war. The previously brave and competent Israelis coward at the sight of Goliath, dubbed a "giant." Indeed, Goliath standing over nine feet tall was a menacing and imposing figure.

The boy, David, had not yet earned a reputation; certainly, not a reputation like King Saul, but David was honing character, along with his skills, protecting his father's sheep. When others, including David's older brothers, trembled at the sight of Goliath, David boldly confronted Goliath. David reduced Goliath's stature by calling him an "uncircumcised Philistine" and prophesized Goliath's demised by attesting that he would "kill him and cut off his head." In modern-day, inner city vernacular, we might say that David was "selling wolf tickets" and we may have further admonished David by telling him "not to allow his mouth write a check that his butt couldn't cash;" however, neither Saul nor David's brothers (who mocked him for being away from the sheep), tried to dissuade David from stepping up to Goliath.

Now, it is important to keep in mind that David didn't have much of a reputation prior to challenging Goliath; yet, all of Israel staked their very lives on the outcome of this battle. The victor would reign supreme over the loser and the loser's people would indenture themselves into lifetime servitude. With all of this on the line, David's older brothers, the Israelis finest warriors and even King Saul, himself, allowed this young shepherd boy to go up against a well-armored, seasoned, nine-foot tall warrior-giant! When David stepped up while others coward, David's character was revealed in that moment and the start of his reputation, unbeknownst to both David and Saul at the time, would eventually rile the king.

Character is revealed in the consistency of one's behaviors over a span of time. David's character grew as a warrior in Saul's command and I can imagine that despite his many victories, it was hard to top the reputation given to him as a "giant-slayer." Reputation (and I would suggest that character, too) can be a fickle thing. We may desire a sterling reputation, but we are not in charge of that and though we are empowered to shape our own character, we can let ourselves down. Saul celebrated David's character when David killed Goliath and lauded his character as an accomplished warrior in Saul's army but what troubled Saul was David's rising reputation. The Israelis heralded David's accomplishments and his reputation outshone Saul's. Envy, jealousy, and anger corrupted Saul's soul and eroded his character. The anointed king of Israel felt his reputation waning, rallied his army to pursue and kill the very man that saved all of Israel when David was a mere boy.

I think that we all like to think that we are better men or better women than we are at times, but I wonder how you or I will behave when our reputation wanes in the sight of others. We don't like to believe that we would have behaved like Saul. After all, he seems rather petty and ungrateful for the services of the young lad that actually saved his reign as king. Of course, we like to think of ourselves having character akin to

David's but how do we respond when our character is assailed? How might a social media post trigger anxiety, depression, or thoughts of paranoia when we presume others are judging us negatively? How might we, like Saul, give credence to an allusive reputation versus building upon our own character? Can we humble ourselves in the presence of a rising star that threatens to dim the glory of the brilliance we once had?

Saul faltered in character with his decision to pursue and kill David; however, David's character was tested again and again, proving the congruence of his reputation earned by defeating Goliath. David knew that Saul was anointed by God to be king and though he was under attack David never chose to retaliate against Saul. Indeed, when Saul was in hot pursuit of David, David entered Saul's camp when he was fast asleep and could have killed Saul but revealed even greater character by not doing so. Your enemy is in your hands. You can squeeze tight and crush the life out of your enemy...do you do it? You can trust in God as your vindicator or expediently tighten your grip and vanquish your enemy in that very moment. Character requires a lot from us, in that we remain steadfast in our principles, integrity, and core beliefs despite fleeting and transitory notions about our reputation.

Ultimately, Saul was wounded in battle but rather than being taken by his enemy, he dies by his own sword and David does assume the role as King of Israel. What we are seeing in many of the biblical stories written are of imperfect, fallible human beings anointed (or chosen by God) to do big things. An often mysterious, idiomatic, and confounding God uses the wayward (The Prodigal Son, Jacob, Jonah, etc.) to carve out a new way. God gives greater value to the widow's mite versus the prosperity of the rich man unable to part with his wealth to enter into Heaven. God uses the courage of a seemingly insignificant boy to do battle with a Philistine giant. Each of these stories is a legacy left for our spiritual edification. These chronicled stories make known the reputation of the individuals and God. Nevertheless, character is forged within the fire of adversity and seasoned over the course of time. David's defeat of Goliath was heroic but David didn't automatically become the boy-king. His character continued to be tested and tried throughout the span of time. Character is not revealed within one single, solitary action but character can certainly be undermined by an incongruent action. I've heard it said that "each of us has integrity until it cost us something" and what we do over time despite the cost will be a testament to our character.

What I enjoy about reading the stories of the Bible, which becomes a "saving grace" for me (and I dare say for you, too), is that God is not looking for imperfect people to be perfect. It is heartening to see heroes of the Bible, striving to obey and honor God, falter along the way. Oh, yes, I love a spiritual exemplar that has paved the way upon this spiritual journey that I am endeavoring to follow, but our mentors have credibility when we are able to see their vulnerabilities along with their efforts made along the spiritual path. Yes, we have Samson slaughtering in battle a thousand men with the jawbone of a donkey, or Moses' staff splits the Red Sea in half or the shepherd boy, David, defeating a menacing giant with a rock and sling, but each revealed human frailties and vulnerabilities.

Samson was gifted with strength unparalleled with any man of his time (and perhaps even since) but he exposed his weakness to the charms of the cunning woman, Delilah, who sold him out for eleven hundred shekels of silver. Some will say that Samson wasn't very bright in that he knew the Philistines were after the source of his strength. He knew that Delilah was a woman of ill-repute. He knew that when he misled Delilah about the source of his strength the Philistines attempted to subdue him based upon the false information he gave to Delilah. Nevertheless, for reasons unknown, Samson tells Delilah the truth about the source of his strength (his hair) and she shears his locks with the Philistines subduing him and gouging out his eyes. Maybe there was something prophetic about Samson getting his eyes gouged out; "he who have eyes to see, see."

Now, before we come down too hard on Samson, ask yourself, "Have you ever fallen in love with someone that just wasn't right for you?" Have you hung in there even when that person has betrayed your trust?" Have you ever, figuratively speaking, had your "eyes gouged out of their sockets" due to being blinded by love? Has your passion placed you into emotional bondage, devastating you so much that you bring everything down upon you; thus, destroying yourself? Well, Samson did and even though his reputation loomed largely, his vulnerability with Delilah impacted his character and caused his demise.

Of course, Moses' life wasn't a bed of roses either. He was born on the "wrong side of the tracks" to parents in servitude of the Egyptians. Moses was marked for death due to the Pharaoh's fear of an emancipator among the ranks of the Israelis being born. Ironically, (or perhaps "consistently" with the confounding mysteries of God) Moses was adopted into the Pharaoh's household to receive favor by the same man whose edict would have Moses killed. As the story goes, Moses discovers his Levite origins in his 40's, behaves reactively, and kills an Egyptian. He is banished from Egypt; thus, reduced to a sheepherder in the clan of Jethro for 40 years. God compels Moses to return to Egypt and command the release of his fellow Israelis. Moses doubted his ability to command anything with an outcast status and speech impediment. This was certainly a man with fragility (identity issues) and vulnerabilities (stuttering) with a dubious reputation and character for the first 80 years of his life.

I've shared above David's plight in dealing with Goliath, the Philistines, and Saul, but his character, too, was challenged when he watched Bathsheba bathing in the nude (voyeurism), using his power of authority to seduce this married woman, impregnating her and orchestrating the death of her husband. One moment of voyeuristic lust redirected David's trajectory from residing within the pure-heart, spiritual realm back to the indifferent-heart, animalistic realm. In some ways, David behaved exactly how Saul had behaved. Saul, out of envy, sought to kill David and David, out of lust, killed Bathsheba's husband, Uriah. Both Saul and David were anointed men of God but their human frailties came forth.

Even though both character and reputation can be fleeting, they are not the same and what matters more is our character. Jesus' reputation was diminished in his hometown *"A prophet is not without honor except in his own town, among his relatives and in his own home."* (Mark 6:4 NLT). Jesus rides into Jerusalem on a donkey during the festival and the people are singing His praises, laying palm branches before Him and in a matter of days, His reputation turns in the mind of the people and they jeer Him as He marches to His death. Jesus' reputation is mercurial (even today with some doubting His divinity or others doubting His existence) but His character remains the same. Christian salvation rests on the character of Christ and not the skewed reputation He had with people of His time or any negative reputation that endures.

I would love to be thought of well. I rather people think of me as being more intelligent than foolish; honorable vs. dishonorable; thoughtful vs. inconsiderate; sincere vs. disingenuous; persevering vs. giving up; determined vs. feckless; supportive vs. uncaring; abiding faith vs. fickle and on and on. Interestingly, when working with clients operating in the indifferent-heart realm, they will adhere to a foolish path that they believe is intelligent. They have misguided notions of honor, perhaps not squealing on the fellow addict that helps to rob your house but they rob your house. They may "thoughtfully" remember to get their paramour a gift on a special day and repeatedly lie to their spouse about having an affair. They may be indignant when you question their sincerity but are disingenuous as the day is long. They pursue wrong-headed ideas and easily give up when a right course is laid out for them. They may speak about their determination to make wrong things right but return to behaviors they'd feel outraged about if you engaged within them. They demand support for their dreams, goals, and activities but are uncaring about how their dreams, goals, or activities impact you. They may loudly boast of their belief in an All-Mighty God but engage in behaviors they know to be ungodly.

The Apostle Paul suggests that we must endure problems and trials as a mark of our character but awareness comes before endurance. We must have the vision to clearly see our character, separate it from our reputation and not simply endure the problem and trials but use this awareness for corrective action that launches us into the pure-heart realm of enlightenment (knowledge plus action). Indeed, the Apostle Paul, when formerly known as Saul, had a fierce reputation as the persecutor of Christians. He had conviction in his zealous pursuits to persecute those he felt deviated from traditional Abrahamic Laws. He was fully convicted in trying to honor the God of Abraham and fully wrong. The pure-heart realm grants us knowledge (awareness) and it is commensurate with appropriate action.

If each of us endeavors to walk a spiritual path, we have to put aside our allegiance to reputation but spend our efforts honing our character. You will not be very popular if you chose not to guzzle beer at a raucous frat-bro party but your character is being "forged in fire" with your ability to say, "No." If the Delilah's of this world titillates your fancies, the honing of your character comes from your ability to resist her seductive charms. As we see above, Godly men have been compromised in their character but God didn't abandon any of them (or will He abandon any of us). God didn't sanction the behaviors that go afoul of His Glory and Design, and He recognizes the fallibility of imperfect human beings. Apostle Paul instructs us that our problems and trials are designed to test our endurance. That is, are we giving up on our path and giving in to temptation, or do we resist this with endurance? Our endurance reveals our character and may ultimately coincide with a favorable reputation but we can only govern the former and allow the latter to take care of itself.

FEEDING THE SPIRIT

Take a moment to reflect upon your reputation. That is, what is the image that you believe that others have of you? Jot down how you believe you are perceived by others. Are you confident or insecure? Are you bold or timid? Are you cool or goofy? Richard Schwartz (IFS) asserts that we have a "self" with a myriad of subpersonalities that are triggered by a host of situations. Invite five people to make a list of five personalities (a total of twenty-five) that you exhibit to them. Conduct a thematic analysis to determine the top five personalities observed by others (and see if they align with your own perception). Use the information to validate your undesirable personalities (i.e., mean, annoying, irresponsible) and augment your desirable personalities (i.e., kindhearted, attentive, responsible).

THE PERSONIFICATION
OF EVIL

**Get behind me Satan! You are an offense to Me, for you are not
mindful of the things of God, but the things of men.
(Matthew 16:23; NKJV)**

At the time of this writing, Donald J. Trump is the president of the United
States. It is my fervent hope that at the time of publication for this book,
the pretend Emperor, who has long revealed that he has no clothes, has
been dethroned. At the very extreme end of the indifferent-heart realm,
I have described in the Fruit of the Spirit, is the personification of evil.
Donald J. Trump is the personification of evil! This is not meant as a
political statement from a "leftist-liberal" as I value many conservative
ideas; indeed, some representatives of conservative ideas, I have a great
affinity for. However, if we don't call something what it truly is, evil
metastasizes and spreads through the world. This is not meant to be a
disparaging of Trump, himself; as, "there but for the Grace of God go I,"
but it is incumbent upon each of us when we see evil to flash a bright light
upon it, as evil grows in the dark.

Prior to the Trump presidency, I was amazed as a black therapist, when
sitting in a session room with some white clients that they felt free to utter
racist, bigoted, and xenophobic rhetoric with impunity. Perhaps (prior to
Trump) the social pressure of political correctness silenced people from
voicing what they authentically felt but this free expression of hatred
spreads just like the Coronavirus. It spreads because the leader of the
United States champion's chaos, delights in divisiveness, and foments

fears. Clients adhere to the clarion call of Trumpism without any critical analysis whatsoever! A delightful, charismatic, Christian, Caucasian client, presenting with anxiety and depression, tells me during one session that she is opting not to seek employment due to the possibility of exposure to someone asymptomatic with the Coronavirus. She then spewed an emotional tirade in a subsequent session that someone dared to confront her about not wearing a face covering while she was in a public venue. It was an incredulous conversation of her extolling her rights to be mask-free to symbolically show her allegiance to Trump with indifference to her Christian values to be in service of fellow human beings.

Lest you think that I'm being too hard on Trump in characterizing him as the personification of evil, let's examine what Christ-Consciousness looks like. The spiritually enlightened, 39th president of the United States, Jimmy Carter, wrote in his book entitled, "Faith", "To me, God is the essence of all that is good, and my faith in God induces a pleasant feeling of responsibility to act accordingly." Trump doesn't act upon what is good and what is Godly; rather, he acts upon self-interest and without any Godly consideration. If we are clear about what Christ-Consciousness is then the antithesis of this would be the personification of evil. The Apostle Paul listed in his epistle to the Galatians very clear attributes of God as the Fruit of the Spirit. I've written about the fruit of the spirit in a similarly entitled book but let's examine them here as they related to this megalomaniac called, "Trump."

Christ embodies love, exemplifies love, and instructed that each of us aspire to this essence of what God is during our individualized walk in life. I have equated "love" to "praxis" (informed action) because love is not willy-nilly or owee-gooey sentiment; it is demonstrable action. It is an action that is well thought through, other-focused, and designed for the betterment of the recipient. If the motive at the heart of any action is designed for self-promotion, self-aggrandizement or self-indulgence, it is not aligned with love. Though this Christ-described love is primarily other-focused, it is important for each of us to genuinely and authentically love ourselves; as it is impossible to give away what we don't possess within ourselves. However, Trump loves money/power/status, his image, and adoration from others, along with the sound of his own voice. Anything he might give is tainted with strings in how the gift can ultimately benefit him.

Perhaps it is not his fault, as no one that originates from the Essence of Love (God), doesn't long to return to that Essence of Love, unless something or someone disrupts the spiritual beings return home. As a therapist, I, too, initially forget at times that the hardened soul of the client who commits an egregious act or engages in exclusionary rhetoric have gaping wounds that remain unhealed that distorts their vision of God and manifests negatively in their behaviors. Love eludes these individuals; yet, the hunger for love remains. The degree of Trump's indifference, disdain, and alienation from others are equal to his desire for love, validation, and appreciation from others. Trump hungers for the love of God but as the personification of evil, he discounts and invalidates everything that God is.

The above client and a whole array of people have aligned themselves with Trump. They, of course, don't see themselves as evil and in aligning with Trump, they don't see him as evil and therein lies the ignorance associated with the indifferent-heart realm. The father, who beats his son as severely as his own father has beaten him, believes he has done no wrong, resides in the indifferent-heart realm. The guy, who yanks his significant other through the window of a car, asserting he has done no wrong because he came to the aide of his child whacked on the butt by his mother for refusing to potty train, resides within the indifferent-heart realm. The woman that stealthily hid a five-year affair from her husband lamenting that the only thing wrong was making the slip up that exposed that affair, resides within the indifferent-heart realm. And, those who associate with those who endorse evil will manifest that evil. The Apostle Paul wrote, *"Do not be deceived: 'Evil company disrupts good habits.' Awake to righteousness, and do not sin; for some do not have the knowledge of God…"* (I Corinthians 13:33; NKJV).

Political pundits and other social media reporters have commented upon Trump's inability to express joy. He has a dour demeanor with no glint of joy in his public persona. Maybe, just maybe, a golden toilet gives Trump joy but I dare say that he is most excited about the notion that others know that he has a golden toilet. He relishes his brand and Trump longs to trump others. However, even if Trump shows demonstrable joy in accumulating wealth, status, and power, these are the attributes of the material world and the antithesis of the Joy in the Lord. *"The humble also shall increase their joy in the Lord. And the poor among men shall rejoice in the Holy One of Israel"* (Isaiah 29:19; NKJV).

When I am speaking to clients that lack joy (often stating that they don't know what it means to be happy) I try to re-conceptualize what this notion of "joy" or "happiness" means. Many of them, like Trump, see joy or happiness resulting from material acquisition. They lament that they don't have the home that they've dreamed about or the income to purchase a new vehicle. They remain sullen in that they don't have the women they hoped for or bemoan the fact that their men have just left them. Their occupation is no longer a calling for them and their community sucks the life right out of them. They perceive joy (happiness) as skiing down mountains of fresh powdered snow, nestling their toes in the warmth of a white-sand beach, or enjoying a disco dance floor on a luxury yacht in the Caribbean but I would dare say that the joy tied to each of these momentary experiences would soon wane if no other activities were to follow.

Dissatisfaction within oneself searches for joy or happiness outside of one's own daily experience. However, a joyful heart finds happiness in a poop-filled diaper of their infant child. Joy oozes out of us when we claim unmerited talent in bowling prowess and our first toss is a gutter ball; causing laughter to fill the room. Joy happens during the early morning, sipping coffee on the patio during a crisp fall morning. Joy is all around us! Joy is within us! Joy is what God is! Joy is what we are! A representative of evil, like Trump and others, divert our attention from focusing on our spiritual essence of joy with the distorted view that this is something apart from us that we must venture elsewhere to obtain.

Trump, the personification of evil, has no peace. He stokes fear and division among people to entertain him. Kids in cages don't cause him to flinch; rather, it is a brainstormed policy initiative that he is proud of. The rise of racist hate groups is not disavowed or tamped down because they grant allegiance and adulation to the wannabe king. Trump is indifferent to the fact that he was impeached by the House of Representatives in Congress and indifferent to the thousands upon thousands he allowed to die during the COVID-19 pandemic. The world despises and disparages Trump. Helium-filled balloons characterizing him as a big baby is how nations aboard view this American president. Trump is indifferent to FBI probes, civil suit allegations about his character, and corruption charges likely to ensue once he leaves office. However, being indifferent toward something doesn't connote that he is at peace. He cannot be at peace because peaceful people have a peaceful countenance; whereas, the restless Trump stirs the pot wherever he goes.

The personification of evil is devoid of goodness and Trump's exploitive, manipulative and corrupt nature doesn't abide in goodness. Goodness is a standard of conduct that God prescribes and Christ exemplifies. Trump doesn't abide in goodness; rather, he ridicules and denounces those who do. He has disparaged the first African-American president (Barak Obama) that has been nothing but the epitome of goodness. He disparaged a man of valor, John McCain who was a captured, tortured war hero who continued service in the United States Senate (until his death). He wasn't present and frankly not welcomed at the funeral of Representative John Lewis, a civil rights icon. There is no goodness in Trump who knows how deadly and transmissible the Coronavirus is, not only hosted an ill-advised rally for his supporters in Oklahoma but discourage masks and removed stickers that informed the crowd about the concerns for social distancing.

Trump, the personification of evil, has no patience. He tweets incessantly and oftentimes inaccurately. He is devoid of an attention span; however, so is the media and so are many of us that follow the media. In many ways, Trump's understanding of the media's lack of sustained focus is strategic. The bad news can't stick, marinate and derail Trump because people shift from one thing to the next and the next. With Trump's impatience, he lashes out his irritation and frustration. It is interesting to see because we know that Trump is a coward; yet, the cowardly in the Republican Party is afraid of the coward. Trump has no patience to persevere because he lacks a vision of God's Goodness to pursue. *"Now may the Lord direct your hearts into the love of God and into the patience of Christ"* (2 Thessalonians 3:5, NKJV).

Trump, the personification of evil, clamors for loyalty but demonstrates no knowledge of faithfulness. "Faith" is not merely the *"substance of things hoped for and the evidence of things not seen"* (Hebrews 11:1; NKJV), it is about fidelity. When we have faith in something, we have trust in it. Those of us that are spiritual-minded trust in the existence of God, trust in His favor, trust in His protection, and trust in His grace. We trust in God's abiding love and we trust in the fact that we are never forsaken. We trust that despite our transgressions we can be redeemed but Trump believes only in himself and he is not even faithful to himself. Over 60,000 mental health professionals signed a petition created by Dr. John Gartner stating that Trump has a serious mental illness that makes him incapable of governance as president of the United States. These professionals were able to see, evident through Trump's own tweets, *"The tongue of the wise uses knowledge rightly. But the mouth of fools pours forth foolishness."* (Proverbs 15:2; NKJV)

Hillary Clinton, in her 2016 presidential campaign coined a phrase, "bucket of deplorables" in referencing the acolytes of the then presidential opponent Trump. Of course, name-calling is beneath those striving to ascend beyond the craving-heart realm and good people opting for a candidate other than Hillary Clinton ought not to be called "deplorable;" however, when I witness others (i.e. Republicans) abandon their fundamental principles to cosign with Trump that seems to be nothing less than deplorable. Their actions are deplorable and Christ would say, "Hypocrites." Christ asserts, *"And whoever exalts himself will be humbled, and he who humbles himself will be exalted. But woe to you, scribes and Pharisees, hypocrites! For you shut up the kingdom of heaven against men; for you neither go in yourselves, nor do you allow those who are entering to go in. Woe to you, scribes and Pharisees, hypocrites! For you devour widows' houses, and for a pretense make long prayers. Therefore you will receive greater condemnation."* (Mathew 23:12-14; NKJV) Christ goes on to say in verse 15, *"Woe to you, scribes and Pharisees, hypocrites! For you travel land and sea to win one proselyte, and when he is won, you make him twice as much a son of hell as yourselves."*

Trump, the personification of evil, has no love; thus, devoid of gentleness and kindness. How does a person look at the shock of a nation after witnessing the needless death of an unarmed and physically restrained black man pour into the streets to register their protest of this inconceivable violent act, to be called, "thugs?" How does the man holding the highest office in the world reference his political opponent's vice-president candidate as "nasty?" This man speaks language with the callousness of his heart. He can't apologize for anything. He can't admit fault. He can't emote or feel the pain of others. He can't comfort others and his praise is often inauthentic. Kindness is not represented in policy when Trump strives to dismantle the Affordable Care Act-Obama Care during the middle of a pandemic.

Trump, the personification of evil, lacks self-control. There are people who foolishly thought that the 2016 candidate Trump's behavior, whose captured words during the Billy Bush interview at Access Hollywood on his crass treatment of women, would magically transform when putting on the mantle of President of the United States. Many gave him a pass for being undisciplined and uncouth. Many held their noses with one hand, while crossing the fingers on their other hand, hoping that a better man existed underneath the brash reality TV personality. What we've learned is that the same undisciplined man, whose sister did homework for him while he was in college, remains an undisciplined man at the end of his first term presidency. He is not different now than what he was projecting then; yet people are surprised. Trump is unable to comport himself differently and Christ spoke of those unable to hear him, "*You are of your father the devil, and the desires of your father you want to do. He was a murderer from the beginning, and does not stand in truth, because there is no truth in him. When he speaks a lie, he speaks from his own resources, for he is a liar and the father of it.*" (John 8:44; NKJV) As of the writing, during this very moment, it has been determined that Trump has lied and/or espoused misinformation at least 20,000 times.

The tendency we have when we label someone as the personification of evil, is that they are an anomaly. We think that they are few and far between and certainly not representative of us. We don't like to think that the same people singing praises to the Lord days earlier were the very same people who crucified Christ. Evil men who ascend to the prominence of political leadership or religious leadership (traditional and/or cult leadership) do so by an enabling followership. I have raised the specter of Trump's evil because he has so many followers. Many of the clients that I serve, as well as many in the rural community in which I reside, and many within the country of my birth (USA) have climbed aboard the "Trump train." They are unapologetic and unmoved in their cult-like following of this evil man.

In the 2020 presidential election, Joe Biden, along with the first female, biracial (black/Indian), vice president candidate earned a record-setting 80+ million votes! What is equally as extraordinary was that there were a record number of votes cast for losing candidate, Trump, whom I equated with evil. As I tried to reconcile how so many people aligned themselves with evil, I was reminded about the lessons I share with my therapy clients, "When knowledge of self is obscured by ignorance, men (and women) behave badly," (Dhammapada). Each and every one of us can be diverted from our path that returns us home to God if we don't apply due diligence. Each of us must be clear about whom we align ourselves with and the direction we are heading. Do we embrace and follow evil out of comfort, familiarity, and expediency or do we do as Christ said to Peter, *"Get behind me Satan?"*

FEEDING THE SPIRIT

Bigotry and hatred are mental constructs resulting from a contaminated spirit, with acts of bigotry and hatred ensuing from our behaviors. For those operating in the indifferent-heart realm, that endorses evil (living life backward due to ignorance), little can be said or done to divert them from their distorted paths. Indeed, they have little appetite to pursue the spiritual fruit that are aspirational for those residing in the craving-heart realm and experiential lived by those in the pure-heart realm. Nevertheless, darkness and light each have its unique allure and to avoid unconsciously slipping into the darkness we must consciously march toward the light. Visualization is a great way to keep the mind honed upon its spiritual essence. Sit daily for 20 minutes with a meditative focus on one of the spiritual fruit. Choose one per month, let's say, "peace," and during the first week of meditation, try to visualize the shape of peace. There will likely not be a static image in your mind about the shape of peace but keep trying to observe it throughout the week. During the following weeks try to visualize the color of peace…the smell of peace…the taste of peace and the sound of peace.

CENTERING OUR THOUGHTS ON GOD

For to be carnally minded is death, but to be spiritually minded is life and peace. Because the carnal mind is enmity against God; for it is not subject to the law of God, nor indeed can it be. So then, those who are in the flesh cannot please God.
(Romans 8:6-8, NKJV)

When I initially engaged in the study of psychology, I was introduced to the three basic schools of thought (i.e., psychoanalytical, cognitive, and behavioral). Others may argue, "What about Wundt and Titchener (Structuralism), James or Dewey (Functionalism), Wertheimer and Kohler (Gestalt), Rogers or Maslow (Humanistic), etc.?" Of course, other great thinkers create other theoretical orientations to assist us in understanding one aspect of our triune self, psyche/mind, but many of the other schools of thought in psychology seems to be a variant of one of the three I've mentioned. It was fascinating learning about the work of the "Father of Psychoanalysis," Sigmund Freud. Whether we are talking about stages of psychosexual development, neuroses, or unconscious processes, Freud's work was really quite brilliant. Of course, Freud had his critics during his time (1890's) and the tweaking of his theories into Neo-Freudianism hasn't really gained much resonance in the mental health community. Psychoanalysis is more theoretical vs. empirical and often ridiculed as a pseudo-science. Likewise, in a puritanical culture our notions of sex was at the forefront of people's neuroses; yet, some might say that even Freud had his own sexual hang-ups as a way of criticizing both the theory and creator of the theory.

The 1950's ushered in an answer to some of the criticism of psychoanalysis with behaviorism from theorists such as Ivan Pavlov and B. F. Skinner where we didn't have to wrestle with this nebulous thing called, "mind;" thus, quantifying empirical observations and reshaping behaviors to obtain a desired effect/outcome. Concepts like operant and classical conditioning entered into the lexicon. Any post-secondary, undergraduate student has likely taken a course in psychology that familiarizes them with Pavlov's salivating dog (pairing feeding with bell ringing and the dog salivates by simply hearing the bell) and the Skinner box (rats motivated to flick a switch for a reward). Instead of a subjective analysis stemming from the client's "aha" response from psychoanalytical/insight therapy, we witness concrete behavioral changes through baselines and measuring devices.

Given that human beings are not "lab rats" or "salivating dogs," in the 1960's we see the role of cognition taking on preeminence in the psychological community. Instead of behavioral manipulation of extinction or reinforcement, or harkening back to childhood and inadvertently shaming mothers for not successfully navigating their children through each of the psychosexual stages, we started concentrating on the cognitions (thoughts) of the "here and now." Sure, the past is important but what are the thoughts in the present that are keeping us stuck or impacting our mental health? Psychologists like Aaron Beck and Albert Ellis focused on thinking errors or distorted thoughts creating our psychological distress. A common statement (Adlerian) that I use with my clients frequently, "It is not so much about what is happening to you in this world, it is how your mind makes meaning of what is happening to you." That is, a loss of a job or broken relationship can be a triggering event that produces opportunity or despair contingent upon how one makes meaning of the triggering event.

Our mind is a powerful thing, but prior to the creation of the discipline of psychology, we were still dealing with the influences of the mind. As Apostle Paul attests above, a carnal mind (relating to the pursuits of the physical body, worldly indulgences, and pleasure pursuits) becomes a pathway to desolation and death. Indeed, Proverbs inform us, *"There is a path before each person that seems right, but it ends in death."* (Proverbs

16:25, NLT) Our effort made in the "renewal of our minds" begins in the craving-heart realm. This is frequently a therapeutic challenge for many therapists (as well as for those sending someone to therapy for a change). We are change agents that change no one! The transactional relationship between God and the client is the therapeutic relationship that produces change. I, as a therapist and spiritual path-pointer, have directed many people on the pathway towards God and many of those experiences were as Solomon expressed "vanities of vanities."

Clients are locked in their intransigence, showing up to therapy for symptom relief (perhaps) but unwilling to change their cognitions or behaviors. As stated in the previous chapter, the antithesis of evil is goodness; thus, the personification of evil represented in a man like Trump is countered by the representative of goodness exemplified in Christ. Some Evangelists, military service personnel, Supreme Court Justices, politicians, and other government officials are pursuing a path that is clearly ungodly. Their intransigence defies logic where people seemingly invest in a candidate that undermines their self-interests. When we incredulously scratch our heads, wondering how this can happen, just recall that throughout history, humanity has behaved in a schizophrenic (split from reality) and borderline personality fashion. That is, they idolize you one minute and denigrate you the next.

Those of us in pursuit of God resist the calling of the flesh and disrupt the appeal of a carnal mind. This is not to say that fallible human beings won't make the mistakes that we've seen with Godly people throughout the Bible but our spiritual transformation will require us centering our thoughts on God. In doing so, I am not suggesting that we become religious zealots. John the Baptist is a venerated Biblical character but he appears to have been a religious zealot. He had an unquestionable devotion to God and paved the way for Jesus Christ's arrival but I don't believe God wants the rest of us to run wild in the wilderness, shouting to others to repent, feasting off of locust and honey. Each of us has a role appropriately designed for the uniqueness of our individual selves. We may be called to a worldwide television ministry or called to simply exemplify our Godly convictions in our daily walk in life.

Centering our thoughts upon God provides a focal point for our progression but we are not to abdicate our human experience. God has granted us, as spiritual beings, the gift to have a human experience; thus, mindfulness and discernment assist us in navigating this material world appropriately. When we are lacking in some area, we must adequately compensate for what is lacking but we must be careful not to overcompensate for our lack. If we break our right arm, perhaps we are right-hand dominant, we'll compensate for our lack of utilization in our right arm by increasing the utilization of our left. If we operate from the perspective, perhaps the fear, that we may reinjure our right arm, we may overcompensate using the left arm even after the right arm has healed. Compensation balances; overcompensating creates imbalance.

Social anxiety develops as an overcompensating reaction to natural fears. That is, safety fears resulting in us having a bit of apprehensiveness among strangers, remind us to be cautious. However, when we overcompensate for our natural precautionary fears, we may become petrified by the familiar faces in our local grocery store. We make erroneous projections that others are in judgment about us. Trauma-induced anxiety may make us a bit wary when we approach the spot that we had our auto accident and we may compensate by avoiding the intersection; however, overcompensation may keep us from ever driving again. Bullies overcompensate for their insecurities, serial daters overcompensate for their lack of intimacy and likewise, religious zealots have a pathological fear of their humanness. With the religious pursuit of zealots throughout history notwithstanding, our journey on this earth is to advance to the pure-heart realm with a cognizant and enhanced relationship with God.

Recall from the previous chapter when I wrote about the "chosen people" a mutual relationship is based upon knowing, trusting, and caring for each other. In "knowing" God requires us to center our thoughts on Him. This knowledge helps us to fortify our faith by trusting God; while our "trust" in God facilitates our "care" (love) exhibited toward God (obedience), toward others (service), and toward ourselves (validating our worth). Failing to do this leaves one exposed to influences of the carnal mind and the carnal mind leads to "death." "What are you talking about, Dr. Al?" I can imagine the reader posing this question, followed by this statement, "I have heard plenty stories of a multiple DWI offenders, obliterated behind the wheel of an auto with a blood alcohol content (BAC) that rivals one with alcohol poisoning, plows headlong into a family of devoted Christians, killing each of them, where he walks away with barely a scratch." It is hard to reconcile these types of injustices leading the good to death and evil to walk away, but don't become narrowly focused on this. The carnally minded alcoholic was spiritually dead prior to getting behind the wheel and the good Christian family whose lives were cut short did not obstruct their immediate return to God's Loving Embrace. God doesn't promise the spiritually minded a life of longevity or one that is adversity free but the spiritually minded is endowed by God's Grace to experience peace despite the atrocities.

"Because the carnal mind is enmity against God; for it is not subject to the law of God, nor indeed can it be." The Apostle Paul is very astute in his letter to the Romans that the carnal mind cannot align with God and is at odds with God as this becomes very clear to me when providing therapy to those who deny God (atheists), unsure about God (agnostics) or don't care about God (indifferent-heart). Some have equated the individualistic "soul" as the triune of mind, emotions, and will that distinguishes us from our "spiritual" essence that goes back to God (and perhaps they are right) but I have not differentiated the spirit from the soul, but seeing our ultimate triune as spirit, mind (which comprises of our mental capacity, emotions and will...is this a soul?) and body. Each operates in unison to allow humanity to exist upon the material world.

All things are comprised of energy; whether it is a blade of grass, insect, rock, rodent, human being, or God. The mind is the repository of information and energy (a byproduct of God). The mind produces energy and is affected by energy. When the brain, which is said to house the mind, is low in energy, it affects the functioning of the mind (i.e. indecisiveness, forgetfulness, difficulties in concentration, moodiness, etc.). When the brain is high in energy we have greater clarity, decisiveness, attentive focus and, emotional regulation). The role of therapists is to assist clients in regulating the flow of information and energy. That is, in the above example, a grieving family member has received the information of their loss, along with the seeming injustice related to the loss, and their flow of energy goes to anger and depression. Talk therapy helps the grieving client to make new meaning about the loss and disrupt the intensity of the thoughts and emotions that may keep them stuck within intense hatred toward the drunk driver and/or God.

The Apostle Paul wrote, *"And do not be conformed to this world, but be transformed by the renewing of your mind, that you may prove what is that good and acceptable and perfect will of God"* (Romans 12:2, NKJV). I have witnessed the transformation of one's thought process (i.e. information and energy) within a singular session of talk therapy. I had a client verbally attack me in session for making what he thought to be a cliché when I echoed what the police and others have said that he was not at fault for the death of a young driver in an accident that he was involved in. He railed at me, perhaps just sick and tired of people trying to assuage his guilt for the accident that occurred because he was present; thus, concluding his physical presence made him responsible.

Remember that I wrote earlier my supposition that we, therapists, change nothing, but God can use our presence to break through the intractability of one's thought process. I've heard a number of times that I have either said the same thing that someone else had said, or what I have said they already knew but in the moment of that therapy session, it resonated for them (the "aha" response). The client couldn't hear the word, "accident" or separate "fault" ascribed to him for merely being present. Nevertheless, I asked the client if he was sitting in his home (physically present), watching his big screen TV and lightning struck his house, or if frayed wires ignited a fire and burned his house to the ground, would he be at fault? Of course not. His mere presence was not the cause of the fire and whether it was an accident or "act of God" (a reference to random natural events that are not orchestrated by God), there is no fault ascribed to him because the incident is devoid of intention or neglect. That's why the incident resulting in the loss of a young life was deemed an "accident" by the police versus "negligent manslaughter" on the part of my client.

For some reason, with no credit being taken by me, that statement freed him (disrupting the information and energy that kept him stuck in his grief) and he was much better after a single session. In similar fashion, but taking longer to do, a woman with her own issues with methamphetamines in the past, found herself intractably fused in a toxic relationship with her drug-using, philandering boyfriend. She wanted to take him back "one more time" because he swears he has changed and pleads to return home. In the session, she was trying to rationalize reasons to allow him to return. None of the previous arguments, pro and cons list, lost custody of their child, or negative feedback from family members to thwart her decision to take him back was changing her decision to bring him back into her life. That is, nothing was changing her thought process until I said (paradoxical intervention), "Oh I get it," (knowing her drug-using past and seeing her codependent relationship as yet another "addictive behavior") "you just want a little bit of meth."

At that moment, she got it! There was a disruption of the information and energy that allows her to consider different options. Perhaps she'll continue down the path of sobriety and awaken to the prospect that she is much greater than what she subjects her life to. Perhaps she'll set her mind upon God and keep it set. Perhaps she'll recognize that God's favor is dispensed upon those who know God. Perhaps, if she continues on the path of spiritual differentiation, she'll invite into her life a guy that values her, supports her, and won't betray her. Renewing the mind is not always instantaneous; it can be incremental and arduous within a therapeutic setting. There is a myriad of therapeutic interventions designed to disrupt the flow of the information and energy that the mind tenaciously grasps ahold of and redirects people to a different life outcome.

In renewing the mind, we realize that "...*those who are in the flesh cannot please God.*" In centering our thoughts on God, our connection with God has as many methods as there are therapeutic approaches and therapy treatments. Common methods of connecting with the Ultimate are dance, worship, meditation, praise, etc. Throughout history and spanning the globe, religious and/or spiritual beings have used prayer as a conduit of information and energy to access the Ultimate in Information and Energy

(God) to replenish the flow of information and energy as spiritual beings renewing our minds. When we beseech God, what are we specifically looking for with the use of prayer? If we are not rubbing the belly of Buddha or Aladdin's lamp for material gain and hedonistic wish fulfillment, what do we seek by prayer?

We pray for wisdom. Through the spiritual conduit of prayer, we are accessing wisdom for discernment and decision-making. The clients that I've mentioned above were disconnected from God's Wisdom and made life choices with a lack of discernment, leading to spiritual death. Spiritual mindfulness garners "life and peace" and we've been instructed to "*choose life that both you and your descendants might live.*" When we tune our ears toward God, we discover, "*For the Lord gives wisdom; From His mouth comes knowledge and understanding,*" (Proverbs 2:6, NKJV). When we pray for God's Wisdom, His Whispered Words come in the stillness of the night in reflective thoughts or dreams. The clarity of His voice comes through in meditation. A "eureka moment" may come through while watching television or listening to the radio. A pastor, therapist, family member, or friend brings forth the answer that we prayed to God for His Intercession.

We pray for meaning in our suffering. Loss can be emotionally gut-wrenching. It disrupts the world we are familiar with, while challenging our sense of stability and faulty notions of permanency. A loss of a loved one, loss of income, or a loss of reputation disrupts our equilibrium and increases neurosis. That is, we will ponder, "Who am I in the space of the loss?" A physiological loss changes our role. We are no longer the mother or father to a deceased child. We are no longer a brother or sister with the departed after a sibling loss. We are no longer a wife or husband stemming from a divorced or deceased spouse. Loss can create suffering (grief) as we attempt to redefine ourselves in the space of the loss. A fractured psyche/soul, resulting from one's loss is repaired when we can tap into God (through prayer) to make meaning of the loss. God can mend our psyche/soul and grant us wisdom and clarity that allows us to make meaning of the loss. Prayer takes us out of our suffering and reconnects us to God's abiding love.

We pray for grace with our affliction. The moment Adam and Eve were expelled from The Garden of Eden, we have had to deal with suffering… we have had to deal with afflictions. God didn't remove Apostle Paul's affliction; indeed, he told Paul that His Grace is sufficient for him. I like this testament in the Bible and this position of God. Miraculous things have and do occur, but we are not always going to be able to barter away our afflictions based upon our petitioning or good deeds. In some ways, all of us have been afflicted by limitations in this world that will create our personal pain. We are limited in wealth, physical attractiveness, health, ability, mobility, friends, family, substance use/abuse, housing, status, and a myriad of other things. These limitations can result in our afflictions but God doesn't always remove the afflictions to keep us mindful in centering our thoughts on God versus ourselves.

We pray for humility. We don't run the show. We never have and we never will. Our existence is a part of God's "Grand ole Design." God grants us an opportunity for this wonderful physical life gift with sentient, autonomy, emotion, cognition, and will. We can arrogantly create a physical life experience that fulfills our sense pleasures or humbly choose God. This is similar to the choices laid out by Satan for Jesus where Jesus could choose the world and everything in it or choose to submit Himself to the Will of God. Jesus fasted and prayed to avoid succumbing to hollow temptations of the world and submitted to God in prayer to remove the "cup" of his impending torture and crucifixion. A prayer of humility reminds us that we know very little and we rely on God's Wisdom to guide us.

We pray to provide praise and worship to God. With truthful admission here, my emotional DNA is more aligned with introversion; thus, dramatic expression of elaborate praise and worship is not my cup of tea. So, I am not inclined to dance in the aisle, with arms outstretched, singing praises of Hallelujah. However, for those who do drop their guard and synchronize their physical beings, and emotional selves with the Light and Sounds of the Most-High God, I tip my hat to them. *"Praise Him with tumbrel and dance; Praise Him with string instruments and flutes! Praise Him with loud cymbals; Praise Him with clashing cymbals! Let everything that has breath praise the Lord. Praise the Lord!"* (Psalms 150: 4-6, NKJV) Nevertheless, we introverts can still praise God with daily recognition and tribute to Him in subdued fashion, as God knows our hearts.

We pray to God for thanksgiving. Gratitude is transformative for the head and heart. It changes a discursive thinking, negativity, and self-indulgent attitude to one with clarity, optimism, and generosity toward others. In thanking God for the little things, we are given more. When we begrudge the things that we have, getting more doesn't satiate us. A prayer of thanksgiving to God reminds us to be thankful for our job, especially with so many people out of work. We are reminded to be thankful for our health; especially while looking around at the random fragility of others. We are reminded to be thankful for the partner that we have, as the one that replaces him or her is likely similarly flawed and the person we've released may be seen as a gem to another. While giving praise and thanksgiving to God, our heart opens up and we are generous to others.

We pray to God for absolution or forgiveness. God is Merciful, Kind, and Generous in Spirit, thus, any petition to God for forgiveness is instantly granted. The slate is immediately wiped clean and a do-over is at hand. We don't have to tap dance, cajole or do penance to obtain God's Forgiveness. God, the Knower of all things, sees a repentant heart even before we utter our petition in prayer but the process is necessary for us as we humble ourselves before the Lord in seeking His Forgiveness for our transgressions. We can't stand before God with arrogance or indifference and expect forgiveness, but there is nothing more we need do but ask (with a sincere heart) and all is forgiven. Just so I am clear here, an appeal to God for absolution of our sins does not abdicate the karmic law of reciprocity; thus, "we reap what we sow" when consequences result from the actions we've chosen. An affair can be forgiven by God and the offended party, but the consequence of the action may still lead to divorce. Murder can be forgiven but the consequence from such action can lead to incarceration. Our prayer for forgiveness releases the mind from the self-indicting guilt and shame, granting grace and peace as we endure the consequences.

We pray to God to enhance interpersonal connections. A prayer for health, blessings, and wellbeing for family, neighbors, colleagues, communities, states, nations, countries, continents, the world, and especially our enemies transforms our sentiment, thoughts, and actions toward others. To harm someone requires us to strip away someone's humanity and spirituality. A word choice that denigrates the status of another (e.g. ethnic, racial, sexist, homophobic, religious, developmental, nationalistic, or any type of slur to reduce one's humanity and deny one's spirituality) creates separation. Separation generates inequitable hierarchies or stratifications. These artificially contrived hierarchies set people against one another and we don't tend to engage with those we don't know or understand. Praying for our enemies lessen enmity, bigotry, and animosity; thereby, eradicating notions of others as enemies.

We pray to God to be replenished. God is All-Encompassing and Fully Sustained. There cannot be anything more than God; otherwise, God cannot be All-Encompassing. There cannot be any diminishing of God; otherwise, God cannot be Fully Sustained. God is the Ultimate Source which all other things spring from. All things that spring from a source are replenished from the source. Just like the flower spreads its petals to receive the warming embrace from the sun, drawing nutrients and moisture from the earth, and is replenished by the source, all things draw its existence from God, The Source. The flower withers when it is deprived of the things that sustain it; as well as we spiritual beings having a human experience withers away when we are deprived of our Ultimate Source. Our prayer to God replenishes the Attributes of God (Fruit of the Spirit) that flows through us and dispensed to others.

We pray to God for attentive focus upon the Spiritual Absolute verse the carnal attractions of the material world. Attentive focus (centering our thoughts on God) provides elucidation (clarity), edification (moral instruction) and enlightenment (awareness plus action). Attentive focus taps into the energy and information that coincides with mind, spirit, and God. Attentive focus is necessary for education, skill development, and ongoing practice. Attentive focus (centering our thoughts on God) not only replenishes the spirit, but also alters our mental processes, and alleviates our mental distress. We can focus on our fears or focus on our faith. What we choose will determine the type of life experience we'll have on this earth.

FEEDING THE SPIRIT

Prayer is a method for directing energy and information toward God and the conduit for receiving reciprocal energy and information from God. It is a spiritual process that has the psychological benefit of cognitive restructuring. Develop a daily prayer life. There doesn't have to be lengthy and elaborate prayers. It doesn't have to be formal prayers. Just start off by simply talking with God

DECONSTRUCTING
THE LORD'S PRAYER

Our Father which art in heaven, Hallowed be thy name.
Thy kingdom come, Thy will be done in earth, as it is in heaven.
Give us this day our daily bread.
And forgive us our debts, as we forgive our debtors.
And lead us not into temptation, but deliver us from evil: For thine
is the kingdom, and the power, and the glory, forever. Amen.
(Matthew 6:9-13 KJV)

For some, the Bible offers statements of incredulity, incomprehensiveness, and outright offense. That is, the Bible is replete with patriarchy, misogyny, oppression, debauchery, incest, adultery, objectification of women, racism, segregation, xenophobia, genocide, infanticide, homicide, war, annihilation and I am just getting started here. Much of what we read about these horrific behaviors in the Bible are practiced by God's "chosen people" (Israelis). Some of these horrific behaviors are seemingly overlooked, endorsed, or directed by God. Following bondage and being stripped of their humanity and dignity for 430 years, the emancipated Israelis exhibited their own inhumane behaviors indicative of xenophobia and genocide. In some ways, the victim becomes the perpetrator and the Israelis appear to be a band of marauders, inflicting carnage in their wake under the auspices of an All-Mighty God.

It is hard for those who are earnestly seeking spiritual mentors or allegories to model their own lives after to reconcile some of the stories from the Bible. How do we reconcile after reading stories from the Bible about the father of our faith, Abraham, basically "pimping out" his wife, Sarah, when he was running scared for his own safety by telling the king that Sarah was his sister? It is challenging for feminists to read of Abraham's nephew, Lot, being spared the annihilation that occurred to the cities of Sodom and Gomorrah offering up his virgin daughters to a debauched crowd seeking to sodomize the two strangers (men) in Lot's home. Do we turn a blind eye to the incestuous relationship occurring when Lot's daughters get him drunk so they can be impregnated by him?

It is hard, within our human understanding, to know that God (the Creator of the Universe and of all people) choose a selected group of people (Israelis) to the exclusion of all others and lead them to an encampment of other human beings with a command to wipe out every living soul, sparing no one. Of course, those who considered themselves as the "chosen people of God" can easily discount and diminish the value and worthiness of others; making it easy to exploit, oppress, and eliminate those "others." We've witnessed cult leaders herald their hierarchical position with a "god" and "lording" over their congregation in the most exploitive ways. They exploit God's reputation for avarice gains and hedonistic pursuits.

The Bible, often referenced as the "greatest story ever told" cannot possibly capture the totality of God's Wisdom. God is incomprehensible to the very limited understanding of even the smartest human beings. There are bold declarations and subtle nuance in how God speaks to His creation. My ignorance is profound! I am fully aware that I possess a "thimbleful of knowledge" and my "thimble" isn't even filled. Nevertheless, we are not exempt from knowing and loving God; nor, knowing and loving others and ourselves. When we read spiritual texts, our understanding of the text will always be contingent upon our level of spiritual differentiation. We are moving from ignorance to awareness toward enlightenment; thus, our knowledge becomes more expansive when heading toward God.

I've shared in previous writings that love is not a gooey feeling the washes over us; rather, it is discernment and action. So, even though my knowledge is limited, my discernment is necessary to be a conveyer of love (God is Love) that I strive to understand and employ. Our discernment is necessary to propel us beyond the indifferent-heart realm to ultimately arrive in the pure-heart realm, *"Folly is joy to him who is destitute of discernment, but a man of understanding walks uprightly"* (Proverbs 15:21, NKJV). Without discernment, we defer our autonomy and agency over to others who are fumbling around in the dark with bold claims that they know the way out of the darkness. Without discernment, we can misinterpret God's Wisdom and adopt a fundamentalist view of spiritual writings that convey an inaccurate historical perspective, corrupt moral or ethical comportment, and distorted prophetic ideas. That is, with enlightened spiritual progression, we don't stone women for moral turpitude when we are aspiring for God's Love. Rather, Jesus conveyed and exemplified love in a way that was much different than the religious zealots of his time and those who continue to persecute others without compassion.

Spiritual discernment is necessary for all things we believe and do, and it is needed within our prayers. Jesus was asked by his disciples to teach them how to pray and He instructed them (and us) not to be pretentious and conspicuous with our prayer life in an attempt to show people how "religious" we are (while ostensibly showing people how much better we are than them). Christ informed us to not engage in repetitive babble that doesn't really convey anything. Rather, we are to go to our private places and give reverence to the Most-High with this succinct prayer that I've cited at the top of this chapter. It's a pithy prayer but packed with a whole lot of valuable nuggets. It is devoid of the ignorance that we might find in the indifferent-heart realm and absent of the intellectualizing that occurs in the craving-heart realm. The prayer reflects the simplicity of truth that is revealed in the pure-heart realm. Let's take a look at it.

"Our Father" is a masculine noun and reinforces traditional patriarchy throughout the ages but God endorses both masculine and feminine attributes. Traditional masculine traits consist of "protector, provider, and leader" while traditionally feminine traits consist of "creator, nurturer, and collaboration." God is a protector, provider, and leader, as well as creator, nurturer, and collaborator." We can see these traits replicated in God's Creation. Even bacteria or viruses do not exist independent of anything but need, an oftentimes unwitting, but cooperative host for its

113

survival. In nature, seeds work in concert with the earth that produces vegetation or fruit that ultimately provides sustenance for every life source. Men deposit "seed" in the womb of women and their joint contributions produces the next generation and beyond. Eve wasn't uniquely created as a separate entity from Adam but as a byproduct of Adam. That suggests that whatever attributes Adam had, Eve possessed. Likewise, whatever attributes Eve had, Adam possessed.

There is no real division here but our patriarchal language can imply a demarcation between people that doesn't really exist. Thus, "Our Father" possesses masculine attributes as a protector, provider, leader, instructor, guide, strength, etc.; while, equally containing feminine attributes of nurturance, creativity, comfort, caring, compassion, and the like. Christ informs us that a "*house divided amongst itself cannot stand*" (Mark 3:25, NKJV); nor can the union of male and female people or masculine and feminine energy stand in opposition to each other. This singular and fully expansive energy that is reduced down and categorized into the language of cultural appeal, "Our Father," is the Ultimate Non-Gendered Progenitor who bestows these attributes equally to a human population and we separate them out. That is the work of ego to separate and draw a distinction between entities and not from the Unifier of the Most-High God.

"*Which art in heaven…*" is the second concept of this prayer that I'd like to look at a bit more closely. The Bible informs us that heaven is a godly realm and is the Kingdom over which God presides. Jesus informs and instructs us to "*…seek first the kingdom of God and His righteousness, and all these things shall be added to you.*" (Matthew 6:33, NKJV) So, what is it that we know about God and this Kingdom of God called, "Heaven?" What we do know about God is that He has no beginning or ending (Infinite Entity). To have an origin of one's existence implies that there is a source or some other force that generates its beginning. Given that God is an Infinite Entity, nothing precedes God or will supersede God. Should God have had His own origin story, He would have had to come from some other Source; thus, God would be a "creation" vs. "Creator." And, as a "creation" that emanates from some other source, suggests no permanency in God because everything that is created is also destroyed.

If we conclude, as I do, that God has no beginning, therefore, no end and is a Creator versus a creation then all things must emanate from God. Therefore, the "Kingdom of God" emanates from God and is indeed God! When we seek the "Kingdom of God" we seek God, Himself, and all of the positive, spiritual attributes (male or female) that represent God. There is no end to the positive attributes of God that we can conceive of even within our limited understanding. The God of Love will have traits attributed to the masculine energy of wisdom, guidance, and discernment; along with traits attributed to the feminine energy of empathy, nurturance, and compassion but none of these attributes trumps those identified by the Apostle Paul in his letter to the Galatians, described as the "Fruit of the Spirit."

The Kingdom of God is God and the attributes of God have been articulated well in the nine spiritual fruit identified by Paul; thus, we are given clarity as to what we are to seek. In the Lord's Prayer, Christ is telling us that we have access to these godly attributes and if that becomes our exclusive focus, everything else we may think we need will be added on to us. It is fanciful to think that Heaven is the spiritual home where God resides and with our departure from our human bodies, we too, will go share the residential home (Heaven) of God's. However, if we think about this more fully, since God is the totality of all things (Omnipresent and Omni-encompassing), He couldn't have an external home in which to live. *"...Behold, heaven and the heaven of heavens cannot contain you..."* (I Kings 8:27, NKJV). If our physical bodies represent the totality of all existence, we don't go to an appendage of the human body to reside. How can the totality of our physical body reside in our big toe? Thus, the Kingdom of God may be a place called, "Heaven," where God will reign but all things are God and not apart from Him.

Jesus tells us in the Lord's Prayer that God's Name is *"Hallowed."* Something "hallowed" is holy, sacred, and set apart from other things. God has numerous names cited throughout the Bible. There is Jehovah Rapha (God the Healer), Abba (Father), El Shaddai (Almighty) and a myriad other names but I like what the name Yahweh represents, "I Am." When God conveys to Moses to tell the enslaved people (Israelis) in Egypt that "I Am" has sent him back to emancipate the people that is powerful in its simplicity. God didn't assert what He "was" (past tense) The Creator and Sustainer of the entire universe. God didn't tell Moses what He "will be" (future tense) The Emancipator for the people of Israel. God told Moses what He "is" (present tense)…"I Am." It really is a brilliant descriptor that will convey the totality of what God is but also a wonderful sentence stem that I have used for clients' affirmation statements. They may write or recite, "I am… courageous, loving, beautiful, smart, prosperous, competent, etc."

Names are important. What other people say about us is important (i.e. reputation). What we say about others is important (i.e. gossip). Word usage is important. God spoke into being the creation of the heavens and the earth, demonstrating how powerful word choice is. "Hallowed be thy name" is showing reverence and respect for the Creator of all things. I try, within my limited and fallible self, to be mindful of my word choices when addressing my "brothers and sisters" who are the "children" of the Most-High God. I confront people's self-denigrating language because their word choice erroneously defines who they are and erroneously prophesizes their future. Limited and fallible people make mistakes, but no one is "stupid." Limited and fallible people make poor life choices, but no one is a "loser." Limited and fallible people have severed relationships, but no one is "worthless."

There was a time in ancient history when God's Name was so revered that few (if any) would utter it. Perhaps the highest of the high priest, segregated from others and prostrated with a mixture of fear and reverence, may have uttered God's Name in a submission prayer to convey the notion of how "hallowed be thy name" but we, humans, have a way of misconstruing things and placing them in extreme categories. Words, names, labels are indeed powerful and each of us must exercise care in our word choices (i.e. blessing and curses are in the tongue), but one cannot have a relationship with the thing that one fears. God is not calling us into subjugation of Him, but into a relationship with Him. We honor God in our reverence and in not being casual in our speech toward Him (or toward each other). Even if we happen to be lacking in our own speech and jokingly referencing to our child, "Oh, you are so stupid," we would likely bristle and prepare to fight the stranger who comments about our child, "Look, that kid's an idiot." "Hallowed" is the reverence we give to God and it should be consciously conveyed in our speech to others.

The Lord's Prayer assures us that God's *Kingdom with come and His Will be done on earth as it is in heaven*. We've discussed what God's Kingdom is. It is synonymous with Himself; which contains many spiritual attributes, with some identified as the "fruit of the spirit." What is God's Will for humanity? Deuteronomy 30:19 (NKJV) tells us, *"I call heaven and earth as witnesses today against you, that I have set before you life and death, blessing and cursing; therefore choose life, that both you and your descendants may live..."* Wow, this is a fantastic warning but what is God's Will? Moses tells us in the first chapter of Genesis that God's Will for human beings is to be "fruitful and multiply."

To be "fruitful" is to be productive. Within our human capacity, we are often charged to produce more but we are compensated with less. The clinic where I work constantly increases productivity demands; thereby, reducing one's capacity to generate a robust merit increase in salary. This is not a specific criticism about the agency where I work but an observation that I see throughout the Country. From a human perspective, it makes sense because there is always tension between the cost of goods and services and what others are willing or capable of paying. Nevertheless, our production of spiritual fruit is not designed for scanty yields. Many people are trapped upon a "treadmill of performance." They want to do more, produce more, and reap the recognition for what they've produced.

God is not concerned about our material productivity. A choice between "life and death, blessings and cursing" equates to the pursuit of mammon or Godly principles and ideas. Luke asserts that one *"cannot serve God and mammon"* (16:13, NKJV). Having described what I believe it means to abide by God's Will to be "fruitful" (productive); the other directive is to "multiply" (expansive). After one develops or produces a yield, it is multiplied by expanding and dispensing the spiritual attributes of God. Mammon doesn't exist in the Kingdom of God so if God's Will is to be done on earth as it is in heaven determines how we are to be "fruitful" upon this earth. Love, peace, joy, patience, kindness, gentleness, faithfulness, goodness, and discipline are the "fruit" God is looking for us to produce and dispense on this earthly plane. Consequentially, Luke informs us that whatever is comprised of God and His Kingdom is represented within ourselves, "*The kingdom of God does not come with observation; nor will they say, 'See here!' or 'See there!' For indeed, the kingdom of God is within you.*" (Luke 17:20 NKJV)

So far, we have been able to deconstruct the Lord's Prayer in what it means about "Our Father" (which is more expansive than our patriarchal notions); the "Kingdom of God" and "God" (synonymous concepts incorporating the attributes of the fruit of the spirit that reside within ourselves); "Hallowed be thy name" (the importance of names and word choices) and the nature of "God's Will" (to be fruitful and multiply). The next portion of the Lord's Prayer is our petition for our "daily bread."

We are spiritual beings having a human experience. To be human versus being strictly spiritual is a gift of sentience (awareness of self), having sensory input, individuality, autonomy (the capacity to choose the direction of our lives), having a complete emotional array and cognitive capacity (sapience), and agency (the capacity to mimic creation and establish connections in order to exhibit and dispense the fruit of the spirit). In the physical world, we can be torn by the pursuit of hedonism and mammon or pursue greater spiritual ideas and hone our faith. Are there angels amongst us? Who am I to say, but angels are "messengers from God" who would lack the autonomy to do anything but God's Will. These "angels" are commissioned by God to carry out His Directive to intercede on behalf of humanity. Unlike Jonah, enlisted by God to be a "messenger," but was not an "angel" because Jonah had the autonomy (and agency) to do the exact opposite of what God commanded him to do.

If God is "Our Father" (encompassing attributes that both males and females will endorse), it goes without saying that we must be His children.

Not unlike human parents who have our own children, we may delight or wince at their experiences in this world, but we don't deny our children what they physically need to exist in this world and neither does "Our Father." *"Give us this day our daily bread"* is not only a petition we ask of God but it is a covenant between a Loving God and His Children. Jesus stated to his disciples, *"If you ask anything in My name, I will do it."* (John 14:14, NKJV) God doesn't require us to purchase, barter, or contract for our daily necessities. The air we breathe, the water we drink, the vegetation grown is the "daily bread" God provides to sustain us within this physical world. Of course, we, human beings, find ways to monetize God's free gifts and disperse this in an unequal fashion that the wealthy remain rich and the poor have trouble breaking free of their impoverished lives.

Nevertheless, God, the Creator of the Universe, recognizes the fact that we are trifold beings (i.e. spiritual, mental, and physical); thus, provides us with the necessities to thrive in each of these areas. *"So don't worry about these things, saying, 'What will we eat? What will we drink? What will we wear?' These things dominate the thoughts of unbelievers, but your heavenly Father already knows all your needs. Seek the Kingdom of God above all else, and live righteously, and he will give you everything you need."* (Matthew 6:31-33, NLT) Given that God has graciously supplied us with everything to meet our needs (daily bread), we are obliged to replicate this graciousness in the lives of others. If you are reading this book and reside in the pure-heart realm, I don't have to tell you about the importance of giving. If you are reading this book, operating from the craving-heart realm, don't allow your intellectualizing and rationalizing to sway you from giving. And, of course, the uninitiated in the indifferent-heart realm are not reading this book and are in hot pursuit of the things that are not of God; which, you and I are not going to be able to talk them out of.

Perhaps it is naivety or perhaps it is pure arrogance that we, human beings, will take the unearned, free gifts and resources of God, manipulate them, repackage them, brand it with our names to sell, barter and contract with others. In Genesis, we are told about Adam and Eve's departure from the Garden of Eden that men shall work from the sweat of their brows to bring fruit from the land and in Thessalonians, Apostle Paul admonished that those who don't work should not eat. So the "bread" is given by God and we have to work to extract the bounty of God's resources but we monetize these gifts and the labor to extract, package and redistribute these gifts to generate profit. Perhaps bartering for goods in the information/technology age is not practical, but how we monetize free gifts and exploit labor goes against spiritual ideals.

"And forgive us our debts, as we forgive our debtors." The forgiveness of our debts is a powerful complement of love. How have we fallen short in the Presence of God every single day? As a young man, encountering the word, "sinner" troubled me. As a therapist, our linguistic reframe changes discursive labels to something more affirming; therefore, less stigmatizing or pathologizing of the individual. That is, "retarded" shifted to "intellectual disability" and instead of referring to someone as the disorder, "He is schizophrenic," we emphasize the "person" who happens to have a disorder ("He is Sam who has schizophrenia."). Likewise, in the culture, an accusatory statement such as, "You are a sinner!" shifts to people being the "fallible children of God who sin." Religion (at times) has been corrosive with its constant drumbeat in devaluing people along the way, and I certainly don't want to endorse this type of devaluation of people. Nevertheless, those proclaiming that we are all sinners speak the truth. If the concept of sin is "turning our backs on God" then no matter how staunchly religious we are, imperfect humans are unable to operate in the physical world without sin. Oh, we may be able to resist doing the big things like adultery or murder but we turn our backs on God in so many little ways that it is impossible to count.

If, despite our best intentions, we are sinning constantly then we need constant forgiveness by God. The Lord's Prayer causes us to be mindful on a daily basis to beseech God's forgiveness that squares us of our debts that we've intentionally, unintentionally, and inevitably make each and every day we draw breath. This forgiveness not only absolves us of our own transgression, but it also models for us what we must do for others, on a daily basis, who has wronged us. Admittedly, I've struggled with these notions and perhaps the reader can help me out. I do believe that it is incumbent upon us all to forgive with the benefit of that forgiveness being an indirect gift to ourselves. However, I have also put forth the notion that forgiveness is a cognitive process that we go through to arrive at a full pardon or amends. This cognitive process involves the steps of clearly assessing the wrongdoing, acknowledging the wrongdoing, sincerely apologizing for the wrongdoing, atoning for the wrongdoing, an offer for amends/pardon for the wrongdoing, and remaining accountable in order not to repeat the wrongdoing. Perhaps I am adhering to my therapeutic process that does take work versus a spiritual process that wipes the slate clean.

Nevertheless, I realize that relationships are transactional. It is represented in the covenant between God and us and the transactions we have with one another. For a contract to be binding there must be a mutual agreement. That is, I cannot impose upon you to pay me thousands of dollars for an old, beat-up jalopy, simply because I say the offer is fair. We haven't established a "meeting of the minds" where we both are in agreement that the item for sale and the monetary exchange is fair. When the agreement is set and a breach occurs, it produces a betrayal in the trust bond that one has with the other. To restore the trust bond, one must go through the steps of forgiveness. If not, there is a relationship imbalance that makes the person who was betrayed susceptible for further betrayals.

A transaction with God is based upon faith, but it is still a transaction based upon the meeting of the minds. Some, in the indifferent-heart realm, doubt that God exists. We can't have a contract with something that we don't believe exists. Moses writes in Deuteronomy 7: 9 (NLT) *"Understand, therefore, that the LORD your God is indeed God. He is the faithful God who keeps his covenant for a thousand generations and lavishes his unfailing love on those who love him and obey his commands."* The demonstration of our faith is through obedience; thus, we are putting into action the very thing that we believe. Additionally, the Apostle Paul asserts, *"Examine yourselves to see if your faith is genuine. Test yourselves. Surely you know that Jesus Christ is among you; if not, you have failed the test of genuine faith."* (2 Corinthians 13:5, NLT)

God is indeed incomprehensible and often counterintuitive, so with my "thimbleful of knowledge" I may be totally missing this concept of forgiveness but even God's Covenant is based upon a contract with believers. Those who don't believe fail to enter into a contract with God and if they have no contract with God, honoring the Lord's Prayer, as it relates to forgiveness may seem a bit empty and less likely to be replicated for others. But if we choose a life of faith, even though we fall short daily, the capacity to forgive is a spiritual gift that we ask of God daily, seek to dispense to others, and to apply to ourselves. In working with clients, the forgiveness of self appears to be the hardest challenge (at times). Sometimes, it is easy to forgive God in the abstract; along with perfunctory forgiveness of others, but many struggle with self-forgiveness.

We see in the 5th line of the Lord's Prayer a petition of God not to "*lead us into temptation, but deliver us from evil*," but this is a bit of a misnomer because God never, ever leads us into temptation. Temptation exists. It tests and refines our character but a Loving and Holy God cannot lead one into temptation. Darkness may be immense but light will always vanquish darkness. Darkness may exist but not in the presence of light. Therefore, a Loving God…a God that cannot abide sin, cannot lead one into darkness. Indeed, the light is present to steer people away from the pitfalls that we were unable to see while existing in darkness. Perhaps we should petition God to cast upon us and our journey the Light of His Brilliance in that we don't stumble in the darkness. This Light and Brilliance of God is the antithesis of darkness and evil, so with the clarity of our vision (and the petition of our prayers), we can be delivered from evil.

The Lord's Prayer concludes with Jesus re-asserting that God is the Kingdom ("*seek first the Kingdom of God*") with power (God is Omnipotent) and glory (awe, brilliance, and light) forever (always was and always will be). Prayer is our method of talking with God. That concentrated energy accesses God's Power in a way that non-believers cannot appreciate. Remember, non-believers don't have a transactional relationship with God with a binding contract. Those who place their faith in science are looking for causal connections; such as when one implements the variable "A" the effect will be "B." In the counterintuitive, spiritual realm of God the least of us become heralded, servants become leaders, and the weak are made powerful. Christ assures us that these same godly principles in Heaven play out on this earthly plane (*"Thy will be done on earth as it is in heaven"*).

FEEDING THE SPIRIT

Once you've gotten up and out of bed in the mornings and before retiring each evening, recite the Lord's Prayer. You are not constrained to this prayer but to develop a habit for a strong prayer life, you can begin with this brief recitation in the mornings and evenings. Having established a ritual of daily prayer, go beyond your mere rote recitation of this prayer. Deconstruct it as I have so that you can establish your own meaning and understanding of what this prayer might mean for you and how it is directing you toward more godly ideas (e.g. Fruit of the Spirit)? Also, write in your journal how those ideas are being manifested in your life (i.e. "be fruitful and multiply).

GOD DOESN'T TEST US BUT WE ARE CONSTANTLY BEING TESTED

And we know that all things work together for good to those who love God, to those who are called according to His purpose. (Romans 8:28; NKJV)

Now I must be careful about the above assertion that "God doesn't test us," because throughout the Bible we can see God testing people. Perhaps the first test mentioned in the Bible is attributed to the first man, Adam. It is a dubious "test" because the allegory of the garden may emphasize "tempting" and "disobedience" versus "testing" but if we were to test Adam and Eve's obedience, they've certainly failed. But let's not quibble as to whether or not this disobedience was a test and look at a very clear test. The first major test we see from God is given to Abraham to test his devotion to God.

Abraham is called to sacrifice the only child, Isaac that he and Sarah bore in their senior years of life. Like most people (not all) Abraham and Sarah longed for an offspring; especially to fulfill the promise of God that Abraham would be the progenitor of many nations. The birth of Isaac is a gift, blessing, and miracle; yet, God was then asking for Isaac back. How does one sacrifice the very thing one wanted the most? Indeed, this becomes a challenge for all of us. Do we sacrifice our love for desserts in order to avoid obesity or diabetes? Do we sacrifice our love of smoking to save our lungs or avoid cancer? Do we sacrifice a toxic relationship with the looming fear of being alone? Abraham is called to the test but the sacrifice goes beyond Abraham. Does Isaac have anything to say? After all, it is his life on the line. What about Sarah's sacrifice? She bore a child at an improbable age and no one asks her if she is OK with Abraham killing off her only child. I'm curious as to what might have become of Abraham if he had returned home having killed Sarah's boy?

We are called repeatedly to sacrifice but is that the test? Does God keep a ledger of the times in which we pass the test and the times in which we fail? If so, it makes sense to me as to why people attribute negative events in their life to the testing of God. People rail at God for intervening or not intervening when negativity enters their life. The drunken driver that slams into your vehicle, survives without a scratch; yet, your infant child, securely fastened in the car seat in the rear of the car, becomes a projectile during the impact and dies without having fully engaged in the fullness of life. The tobacco smoking, alcohol swilling, profanity-laced atheist lives to a ripe old age and the pious living, teetotaler, service providing Christian is riddled with life calamities and an early death.

Is God testing the Christian and giving the pagan a pass? Does an Omniscient God, Knower of all things, need to test the resolve of people? *"Let no one say when he is tempted, 'I am tempted by God'; for God cannot be tempted by evil, nor does He Himself tempt anyone."* (James 1:13, NKJV). So, are we tempted? You bet! Are we tested? Every day; however, God is not creating these tests for us or trying to tempt us. Today, I have been tempted and tested but I realize that it is not of God. Today, as a black male in a largely white and rural community, I had arranged to have my oil changed and tires rotated. I had a 9 am appointment but was told to arrive 15 minutes early and stay in the car (due to COVID-19 concerns). They did some basic checks and gathered some information while I was still in the car. I pulled into the bay and with my face-covering in place, I was told that I could wait in the lobby and they would come to get me once the service was completed. After 20 minutes, the lobby started to fill with a couple and two other individuals receiving service.

An hour and a half had gone by with me patiently waiting on my car. I found it a little easier to wait when I overheard a salesperson greeting one of the customers, telling him how busy they've been and even though she worked there, she couldn't get in for service for two weeks. A tech came in to tell me about some challenges they've had with a car that has put them behind and confirmed my service request (oil change and rotation of tires). He implied that he was just now getting to my vehicle and expressed that it should be another "few minutes." I asked what a "few minutes" might mean and he thought it would be another half hour.

Time proceeded and my patience was still unperturbed, until each and every one of the white customers who arrived after I have departed with their cars' serviced. I wondered if this was just another one of those life tests. It is easy to have patience when patience isn't tested. Indeed, as someone who facilitates an anger management therapy group, I've frequently talked about anger stems from failed expectations and perception of disempowerment. The circumstances of our lives are often outside of our control but we are capable of governing the emotional response we have about the circumstances. I also challenge the clients to not make negative assumptions about the circumstance (unless they've checked it out).

My observations were clear. I had to wait and other people...white people... were preceding me. Nevertheless, I was successfully passing the test until such time when I was leaving in my serviced vehicle and my right front tire nearly fell off. I hadn't driven too far when a terrible grinding sound brought me to a halt. When I investigated, none of the bolts were present and I walked back to the service center in a huff, collecting the bolts on the ground as I returned. My thoughts roiled with the notion that I could have been jetting down the highway and the wheel comes off. Who does such a thing; and, was it deliberate? Was this an extension of what was happening earlier, confirming racial animus, or was it just a series of indifference and incompetence?

My patience was tested and my temper was tempted. I did tell an apologetic manager that I was angry with my experience. It is important to identify one's emotion and even express one's anger without allowing the emotion to take over us with verbal abuse, character assassinating or physically attacking others. To that end, I've passed my test, but again the test wasn't imposed upon me by God. It wasn't God that delayed my service. It wasn't God that had others precede me in service who happened to be white (I want to be careful not to conclude that there was any racial animus because at times some occurrences are truly not about race). It wasn't God that didn't secure the bolts on my wheel. So, my patience was indeed tested but it wasn't God designing this as a test to see whether or not I would fail.

When we read the Book of Job, we see the interplay between God and Satan to test Job's resolve, where God certainly seems complicit in Job's suffering. We don't know who wrote the Book of Job. Perhaps it was Job. Perhaps it was Moses. Perhaps it was one of the characters in the exchange, Elihu. Perhaps it was the collaborative work of multiple writers. We just don't know. And, when I reference within my written books that the storehouse of my knowledge would not fill a thimble, it is certainly true when I am trying to understand the Book of Job. The book seems to be an anomaly or outlier when we consider the overall makeup of the biblical texts. It is not necessarily a historical account, so if Moses did write the book, the compilers of the Bible may have appropriately not considered it as part of the Pentateuch. It is not a book of prophecy as a prelude to Christ. It is not an account of Christ or the "Good News" in reference to the New Testament.

The Book of Job (and some have associated the Book as a stage performance, not unlike the works of Shakespeare) focuses on a righteous man (Job) and the meaning of suffering with no real clear answers as I read the text. The argument made by Job's friends (in many ways, great friends who've come to Job to commiserate in his loss and sat in silence, just being in the presence of Job for seven days), turns accusatory in blaming Job for his suffering. With his wealth depleting, health deteriorating and family wiped out, Job's friends (Eliphaz, Bildad, Zopher) and ultimately, Elihu, conclude that Job's unacknowledged sin created his disfavor in the eyes of God. The legacy of this interaction is the "go-to" response that we continue to have in "blaming the victim." Indeed Job's wife confronts Job with, *"Do you still hold fast to your integrity? Curse God and die!"* (Job 2:9, NKJV).

Clients are singing the same song of woe that God is punishing them with unsupportive family members and friends indicting them for God's punishment. They lose a job and ponder whether it is God that punishes them. They suffer from a miscarriage or the loss of an innocent child with internalized anger, grief, or blaming God for their experiences. Some construe the travesties that they suffer as a test but what is the test? Likewise, what was the test for Job? Satan, the archetype of lies, comes before God with a proposition to "torment" ("test") Job. Who is the test for? Is it for God, whose Infinite Knowledge knows the outcome of any such test? Was the test for Satan? We have people during this very moment in time that have been stricken with the Coronavirus, recovering having endured unconsciousness and weeks on a respirator, who have actually had family members and friends die of the virus, continue to align themselves with whom I've dubbed, "The personification of evil," who continue to assert that the virus is a hoax. God must know that tormenting Job does nothing for changing the mind and mission of Satan.

Was the test for Job, himself? Why? When the travesties unfolded, Job lamented his very own birth, but he never denied God and of course, God would know that. Job wanted his righteousness to be put on trial. If his actions, inactions, or unknown actions have caused offense to God, Job wanted it revealed. Job appeared to be willing to stipulate his "guilt" to his friends if some misdeed on his part was the causal factor for his severe punishment, but he wasn't prepared to simply acquiesce without proof. Job's appeal for a trial appears to put God on trial and with umbrage, God chastises Job. God puts on his prosecutorial hat and indicts Job for his ignorance, "*Where were you when I laid the foundations of the earth? Tell Me, if you have understanding.*" (Job 38:4, NKJV). Of course, if one is debating God, it is best to do as Job did and remain silent, but I still couldn't see in God's retort a rationale for Him to entertain Satan and to test Job.

Was the test for the rest of us? Why? Human behavior is fickle. Some maintain resolute faith in the face of travesties; whereas, others did what Job's wife commanded, to "Curse God and die." The Book of Job reinforces notions that I don't believe are true. A wrathful, temperamental, judgmental, punitive, and fickle God that we see in the Old Testament appears to retain His capricious nature within the Book of Job in that "I do what I want and you don't have a right to question me about it." Ultimately, this is true, as why must the Creator have to explain anything to the created? But, even within our human relationships, "Because I said so," is not a cogent response.

Tests are not relevant for God and a Loving God doesn't throw obstacles or travesties in our way to derail our progress or to facilitate our growth. God, whether individually or in cahoots with another entity, devise tests to produce harm in our lives. God doesn't hook us on crack, cause our car accidents, or take away a child at birth. The silly notions that accompany an unexpected loss of people (e.g. "God must have needed a violinist in Heaven to have taken her so young"), make God seem arbitrary, needy, and small. God doesn't create children with cleft lips, Down's syndrome, or with Sickle Cell Anemia. God doesn't create poverty or plagues. God doesn't divvy up the resources and place wealth in the hands of a select few and impoverish the rest. God doesn't take a talented singer, dancer, or violinist as a test for us who remain.

The tests that do occur (but not orchestrated by God) are commensurate with the limitations that each of us will all face within our lived experiences. Again, God didn't loosen the bolts on my car's wheel or caused someone else to do so in order to orchestrate a test for me. Nevertheless, the experience itself was a test for me to determine (for me) my level of spiritual differentiation. Did I lose my faith? Of course not. Everything I know to be true about God before the incident remains true after the incident. Even if the incident was deliberate and racially motivated, does it test my love for whites? Of course not. Even within a country that has imposed legal sanctions and cultural impediments to segregate majority/minority races, I have been uplifted, supported, nurtured, cared for, educated, ministered to, and equally loved by my white brothers and sisters that this incident doesn't taint my capacity to love them back.

Given that forgiveness is not a declared fruit of the spirit articulated by the Apostle Paul in his letter to the Galatians, I tend to incorporate forgiveness with the fruit of the spirit, patience. Losing one's wheel does test one's resolve but my patience/forgiveness remains intact. This patience comes from adherence to standards (goodness). I do have core beliefs that the spiritual essence of all human beings is goodness. If I was deliberately treated unfairly, this is not an indictment of goodness but our core of goodness is tempered by the darkness of ignorance. Perhaps, if the incident was deliberate, the service technician couldn't see himself within me and plotted to do me wrong, but the test for me is to be able to see myself within him and not cause him harm.

It is hard to experience joy when adversities befall us but the test is not to allow the adversities of the world to rob us of our joy. The Apostle Paul has encouraged us to treat it all as joy when we experience trials. The test allows us to change our cognition with the knowledge that it is not so much what happens to us in this world but how our minds deal with what has happened. I can internalize this incident and make it about me or I can keep it external, realizing that I am in the world but not of the world; thereby, returning my trust to God and not let the antics of someone's bad behavior steal my joy.

Peace...equipoise is tested by stress or distress that occurs on a daily basis. Problems enter into our psychological space to disrupt our peace. I speculated why I had to wait in the lobby of the auto dealership to receive the service that I had set an appointment for, but I had taken the day off, brought along my book to read, and didn't allow the inordinate wait to disrupt my peace. Of course, my mood was challenged when it seemed that they were ratcheting up my discomfort by not appropriately bolting the nuts on my wheel. Having a peaceful countenance is a practice that one develops prior to encountering a distressing event. Meditation, prayer, personal reflection, journaling, etc., helps us to maintain our peace when an unpredictable incident occurs; thus, passing the test for this particular fruit.

The methods that I have referenced to maintain my peace are related to self-control or discipline. Indeed, all of the fruit of the spirit requires self-control or discipline. We must discern the type of fruit that we decide to plant, cultivate those plants and dispense the produce of those plants appropriately. Whatever fruit that we are trying to cultivate there will be "tests" in place to keep us from bearing fruit. Some might say that it is the imposition of Satan that disrupts our production of fruit. I'm ok if you need a scapegoat for your lack of fruit production but I recognize my responsibilities for honing the comportment of our behaviors with self-control or discipline. God has bestowed up me (and you) autonomy and agency; along with the wisdom to determine the choices I make when faced with a challenging circumstance and I need not blame God or Satan for it.

Satan's torment of Job, making him financially destitute, physiologically afflicted, and experiencing incomprehensible grief of losing each and every one of his children can affect one's temperament. *"May the day perish on which I was born, and the night in which it was said, 'A male child is conceived.'"* (Job 3:3, NKJV) I think about the many suicidal clients I have known that have said similar things. It is hard to argue that things will get better when people are in the midst of their despair. It is hard to pass the test of kindness and gentleness when nothing else matters. I try to encourage clients to change their harsh and negatively skewed language to generate hope but when one is in the midst of despair the fruit of kindness and gentleness appears beyond their grasp.

If kindness is action and gentleness is the tenor in which kindness is dispensed, it is a challenge to get these clients who have adopted the perspective of Job to direct these fruit to themselves and others. Within my therapy capacity, I confront derisive rhetoric and model optimism, while attempting to reframe negative perceptions. I try to encourage them to shift competencies in that if COVID-19 has stymied one's capacity to work outside of the home, why not become a good partner and parent within the home? If you can't make a business deal because the economy has stalled, why not put efforts in tackling home projects that you never found the time to tackle previously? If one cannot find a reason to be kind to him or herself, why not find a way to serve a meal, sew a mask or make a call to another who is isolated and discouraged by this dreaded virus?

Jobs story is alive and continues to resonate in the lives of so many people knocked off their feet by unforeseen or unrelenting circumstances. If God allows Satan to mess in our lives, then God is culpable. So is there an entity called, "Satan" creating chaos in the world and havoc in our lives or is this simply our internal projections as we attempt to make sense out of what appears to be nonsense? In a bifurcated world when ups have downs, ins have outs and good is contrasted by evil, it is tempting to defer our bad experiences to an evil entity but we have both the disciple James and the Apostle Paul telling us to count our trials as joy, for they teach us something (namely patience or endurance). I remain perplexed about Job's lesson, but generally speaking, because we live, we are constantly being tested by life's limitations, but we can rise up to meet these tests squarely versus finding fault in God who is not imposing these tests upon us.

FEEDING THE SPIRIT

There will be many times during our trek to wholeness that we will be tested and challenged by the events of this world. Losses, betrayals, and putdowns will be a continual life experience that we will have to endure. We can regulate our emotional and spiritual selves with a simple and daily practice of the "open palms" technique. While standing or sitting, turn the palms outward (with your fingers gently cupped upward) in order to receive and release. We can receive God's Love, Mercy, Kindness, etc. and we can release, anger, jealousy, fear, etc. At the top of each hour engage in the open palms technique with a simple recitation of "God, fill me with your _____. And I release to you my_____." This can be done for as little as 15 seconds and up to a minute. You can be demonstrative in your gestures and audible in your recitations (if privacy permits), or inconspicuously turning the palms outward and silently making your recitations (to avoid being a public spectacle).

YAHWEH VS. BAAL

Then Jezebel sent a messenger to Elijah, saying, 'So let the gods do to me, and more also, if I do not make your life as the life of one of them by tomorrow about this time.'
I Kings 19:2 (NKJV)

As a therapist, I find Elijah's story an interesting one. He is a prophet that is so revered that he doesn't simply die off, leaving us the legacy of his lived story through the collective chronicles of fellow prophets illustrated in the Bible, but he uniquely ascends to heaven in a fiery chariot. Not even Christ had the good fortune of ascending into heaven without having experienced death. That is remarkable and those serving the false god, Baal, witnessed Elijah's successful "exhibition" between the Absolute God, Yahweh ("I AM"), and a contrived god (Baal). Jezebel, as a Canaanite woman, marries an Israeli ruler, Ahab, brings her influences of the pagan god, Baal, to the consciousness of Israelis. Her effort to sway the Israeli people from their Singular God wasn't by subtle cajoling or a convincing intellectual argument, it was through violent imposition with Israeli prophets being executed. Elijah lamented, "...*I alone am left the prophet of the Lord; but Baal's prophets are four hundred and fifty men*" (I Kings 18:22, NKJV).

Jezebel's tyranny, Ahab's indifference, and impotence, along with the influences of the false god, Baal, was like a contagion spreading through this band of God's chosen people. Elijah proposed a competition to confront the false god, Baal, head-on. The competition Elijah proposed was designed to turn those who have embraced the false god, Baal, back to believing in the monotheistic God of Abraham. In essence, the competition comprised of two dressed bulls, two altars, and two opportunities to have each "deity" ignite the wood at the altar and roast the bull (without human intervention). The prophets of Baal went first to no avail and Elijah, with total confidence in his God, offered up the handicap of dousing the wood on his alter four times prior to beseeching the Lord to ignite it. Elijah's God showed up and showed out by not simply igniting soaked wood but by burning everything to the ground!

It is curious to see the Israeli's feckless commitment to the God who has chosen them repeatedly as depicted in a number of different trials we read about throughout the Bible. It is curious to see people's feckless commitment to God when people in the 21st Century choose false religious and political prophets over the Universal God that has chosen us. It is curious to see even Elijah's feckless commitment to God when he is confronted by the false god within his own mind called, "fear." Elijah has resurrected a deceased child, performed miracles, exposed a false god, ascended into the heavens without experiencing death, was thought to be the Messiah, himself, when Jesus came upon the scene, and yet, he reacts in a puzzling way, when a pagan woman (yes, considered "wicked") makes an idle threat, causing this man of courage to flee and this man of faith to become gripped by depression. What was that about? Was Elijah really in fear of Jezebel? And, if Jezebel was out to kill him, why not succumb to her in proud defiance (as Daniel has done when tossed in the lions' pit) versus asking God to kill him?

I think that what is glossed over in our readings is that Elijah, in vindicating the Lord, took out his sword and killed 450 men. It is not like a military officer making a command decision at NORAD to launch a missile from a high flying drone in the Middle East at an enemy combatant. Yes, those killed by Elijah were the purveyors of a false deity that redirects the chosen people's path away from God, but killing is killing and far more traumatic when up close than afar. Was it really about Jezebel's empty threats that caused Elijah to flee or was it exactly what Elijah said, *"It is enough! Now, Lord, take my life, for I am no better than my fathers!"* (I Kings 19:4, NKJV) Is Elijah, a prophet, experiencing burnout or has he been traumatized by his very actions? "Yes, God, You showed up and showed out during the competition between You and Baal, but it was Elijah that took it upon himself to kill all of those men." Just so we are clear, Elijah's actions didn't bring disfavor in the "Eyes of God," but it took a toll on Elijah.

What I have gleaned from Elijah's story is that if we overinvest in what we are slated to do, even if it is our calling that is ordained by God, it can tax our soul, burn us out and foment our depression. The emotional toll this ordeal took on Elijah has him collapsed under a broom tree with no desire to go on. God dispatched an angel to nudge Elijah from his sleep, gave him food, and water, and allowed him to return to rest. The angel nudged Elijah again and provided him with food and water once more. This is so important for those dealing with depression; hydration, nutrition, and rest. Given that all emotions serve an important function for our human experience upon this earthly plane, I share with clients that depression is an adaptive emotion that can also serve us. Depression is an internalized "time out" for the mind, body, and spirit that let us know that we are not living a congruent life of integrity.

God truly doesn't give us more than we can handle because all things are within our power when we are aligned with God. If we reside in a Godly constructed universe and a socially constructed world, we have the capacity to construct (and reconstruct) meaning out of our experiences. We can be uplifted by a seemingly deflating experience or devastated by an otherwise positive experience, contingent upon the meaning we make of the experience. That is, celebrity status, a winning lottery ticket, or a million-dollar mansion may ultimately produce depression; whereas, a handmade birthday card from a child, securing a parking spot in front of the store, and watching the sunset with a paramour may produce great joy. We are co-creators of the micro-universe of our individualistic sphere of influence; thus, empowered to create its meaning.

When Elijah was feeling better (what a difference rest, water, food, and movement makes on depression) he seemed to struggle with a basic (yet profound) question God asked of him, *"What are you doing here, Elijah?"* (I Kings 19:13, NKJV). I hate to frame the lamentations of Elijah (one of God's more favored prophets) as a "victim story" but I can still hear the negative attributions of his trauma revealed in his response to God, *"…I have been very zealous for the Lord God of hosts; because the children of Israel have forsaken Your covenant, torn down Your altars, and killed Your prophets with the sword. I alone am left: and they seek to take my life,"* (19:14). He felt overly taxed, all alone and despair. Ultimately, God gives Elijah an assistant, Elisha, anoints another prophet to relieve Elijah and whisks him away in a fiery chariot.

God seemed to be asking Elijah the question, "What are you doing here, Elijah?" as a way to jog his memory as to "why" he is here; which becomes a "meaning" question. When we lose the vision as to "why" we are here we can be overly invested...zealous in our performance, expending more resources than we have and oftentimes even more than what we are required to give. Those in the helping profession (especially now with the ravishing COVID-19 virus on frontline workers) have to wrestle with that question and endeavor not to become overly taxed. Of course, there are institutions (e.g. hospitals, prisons, or schools), companies (e.g. meatpackers, retailers, or grocery stores), and agencies (e.g. mental health, social services, or daycares) whose workers may face mandates for their increased production with a reduction of staff but there are many martyrs in these groups as well. We may turn a 10-hour shift into a 12 or 15-hour shift or turn a schedule 4-5 day week into a 6-7 day week because we feel indispensable. We may forego our breaks or forego a directive to take some time off due to our own zeal.

The propensity to overdo it has been an issue for Americans long before the Coronavirus outbreak, thus, job dissatisfaction, burnout, and depression is an ongoing challenge that we'll need to rein in. The story of Elijah also reveals to me how disillusionment can also occur within the pure-heart realm if we don't stay vigilant. How does the pagan god, Baal, enter into the consciousness of the Israeli people when they have had a direct and substantial relationship with the One and Only God? Baal, the god of fertility, earth, war, etc. was a god venerated by the Canaanites, which is Jezebel's ancestry, who married into Israeli culture, to Ahab and lest you think was the only Israeli affected by outside influences, remember that the wisest man in the world, to whom God granted his request for wisdom, adopted pagan influences, worshiped pagan idols.

Of course, we know that Solomon was disillusioned. With wisdom, wealth, and a thousand sexual partners (700 wives and 300 concubines), he thought it all to be "vanity of vanities," but why are we seeing those who depart from something "true" to adopting something "false?" Perhaps the answer to my question is embodied in Elijah's contest between Baal and God. Baal represents the fertility of crops (during an agricultural era) and fertility of people (where the number of children was representative of one's wealth). Nevertheless, God has "given birth" to the creation of the entire universe! The earth is tangible and present; whereas the notion of heaven is abstract and future-oriented. Baal, the idol, has substance and form that is tactile and visible; whereas, God is ethereal and imperceptible to human senses. Those victimized in a battered relationship will desperately hold on to the "concrete certainty" of the battered relationship that is "real" for them versus risking the uncertainty of an "ideal" relationship that "may" come along.

That constant tug between passion and principles, what is known by empirical measures and what is unknown through spiritual mysticism, along with the concrete, hedonistic appeal of mammon and the pursuit of abstract godly ideals can send us into an emotional, psychological or spiritual tizzy. Our trek toward wholeness that results in self-actualization (realizing one's true self), integrity (pulling together our disparate pieces into a concentrated whole with total self-acceptance) and competency (having sufficient internal resources to deal with external demands) can be thwarted when we lose our vision and motivation to return home to God. We become frozen in our inertia; perhaps crying out like Christ, "My God, my God, why have you forsaken me?"

God told Elijah that He wasn't in the strong wind that tore the mountain into pieces. He wasn't in the earth that quakes. Nor was He in the fire (that burns and destroys) but He was in the small, whispered voice. God referenced three of the five physical elements that He was not a part of (earth, wind, and fire). Of course, all of these elements must be within God (including the other two elements of void and water), because all things come from God but I surmise that the point God was trying to make to Elijah that Baal represented the earth for the Canaanites and God wasn't a part of that. God granted Elijah a reprieve from the challenging ordeal he faced in the material world but what is the lesson that the rest of us might learn from Elijah's ordeal?

Depression, disillusionment, fear, burnout, or whatever disabling emotion we have is a part of our human emotional repertoire that even those in the pure-heart realm will experience. Christ wept. Christ displayed anger (overturning the tables at the temple). Christ expressed exasperation that His disciples couldn't stay awake while He was sweating blood, as He contemplated His fate. Elijah cried out in despair because he had enough and each of us may experience a time that life feels like it is just too much. I have worked with clients and have had enough. I have taught students at a great university and have had enough. I have lead managers, supervisors, and staff as a director of social services and have had enough. I have had compromising health, financial struggles, and relationship turmoil and just like Elijah who ran from Jezebel, I have had enough (at times). We cry out in anguish to a comforting God for His loving grace and mercy to fill our depleted souls.

When depression looms, we have lost our way, and from a therapeutic perspective, we address four domains to revitalize depressed individuals. That is, we address behavioral comportment and physiological changes. This is akin to the care Elijah received when God directed His angel to minister to Elijah's physical wellbeing with rest, food, drink, and movement. I coax clients to eat despite having no appetite, to hydrate with water (avoiding caffeine and alcohol), adhere to a structure of rest, getting out of bed in the mornings, attend to hygiene and engage in movement). Therapists address one's cognitive domain in reframing or restructuring the automatic negative thoughts that lead to a depressive state. Therefore, I challenge self-defeating thoughts and negative word choices of "I can't" or "nothing ever works out for me." Therapists address affect (emotional) regulation to disrupt crying jags, emotional outbursts, and mood volatility. In doing so, I validate tears as therapeutic but implement grounding techniques to disrupt one's overindulgence in raw emotions. And, spirituality inclined therapists, like myself, address the existential or spiritual domains of clients to examine and uproot negative core beliefs/

meaning; thereby, reseeding their "spiritual soil" with fresh ideas to direct them back toward God.

Baal is an idol that represented specific elements of nature that the Canaanites valued (i.e. fertility) but in a broader sense, all idols divert one's attention from the Singular God that creates all of what we are and all of what we know. The "Jezebel's of the world" will try to impose their views upon us to convince us to follow their idols. This is not unlike the drug pusher that coaxes us into drug use or the gang leader that gives an ultimatum to join the gang or die in a hail of bullets, or a president that has us compromise our principles to avoid the sting of a wayward tweet. Baal fertilizes the mind with distortions and lies; while the adherents (or henchmen, like Jezebel or Donald Trump) terrorize others into following false ideas. It was perplexing to see that in the many generations before Christ that the "chosen people" would choose Baal over God due to the fear of one woman. It is equally perplexing that in the Twenty-first Century, the self-confessed children of a Christian god would choose Baal over God due to the fear of one man.

The emperor without clothes has beguiled the American public with a large part of the Country bowing before the golden effigy of the most corrupt president in America's history. When we cease to have steadfast allegiance to the Most-High God, we can quickly lose our way. Indeed, we are told that the path to heaven is a narrow one. Let's look at what Mathew wrote about this, *"Enter by the narrow gate; for wide is the gate and broad is the way that leads to destruction, and there are many that go in by it. Because narrow is the gate and difficult is the way that leads to life, and there are few who find it"* (Matthew 7:13-14, NKJV). It takes desire (willfulness), vigilance (mindful awareness), and discipline (effort) not to succumb to the masses and follow the "Baal's" of this world down a dark and encompassing path. Unlike the depiction of God in the Old Testament Bible, God is not going to impose anything upon us. And, in taking my lead from my notions of God, I am not imposing therapy upon those I know to be wounded or broken and I won't drag a person down the path of spiritual enlightenment.

A delightful young lady, whose face lights up in session, with an attentive focus on the psychoeducational information related to anger management, relapsed on methamphetamines (allegiance to "Baal"), returned to complete her anger management requirements. Prior to her relapse, she expressed enthusiasm about the sessions while denying that she had an anger management problem. Since her return, she was more transparent about her history of anger, and a bit testy in the session. She expressed, "I heard that anger management therapy doesn't work anyway." Research suggests that anger management therapy programs have a seventy-five percent efficacy rate with the incorporation of stress inoculation, arousal reduction, problem-solving, conflict resolution, emotion recognition, cognitive restructuring, assertiveness training, testimonials, modeling, rehearsals, etc. However, the client was absolutely right with her notions about the efficacy of the program (or any program for that matter) that they don't work. Indeed, her treatment programs had little efficacy with her relapse on methamphetamines, so treatment programs don't work either.

Schools don't work, financial institutions don't work, prisons don't work, religions don't work, marriages don't work, and nothing outside of our willingness, awareness, and effort will work for the advancement of each of us. Without this personal investment, nothing, not even God Himself, will unseat His gift of autonomy to work against our desire, vigilance, and effort. Our covenant relationship with God was ordained by God but our choice for a collaborative relationship with God starts and ends with us. It's Yahweh versus Baal and each of us will choose. Should we choose God, we must remain vigilant, as subtle notions, behaviors or interactions can divert us from our "narrow path." The path is not obscure because the God of Brilliance/Light is not trying to hide anything from us, but effort/discipline is necessary for us to tread the path leading us back home to God.

FEEDING THE SPIRIT

Let's try a left-brain, right-brain exercise to tamp down dysregulated emotions and disrupt discursive thoughts. The left-brain is considered precise, organized, logical, methodical, disciplined, meticulous, analytical, etc. Our ability to reason is borne out in the left-brain hemisphere. The right-brain is the flip side with creativity, imagination, spontaneity, artistic expression, and related to the emotional side of ourselves. The following steps will help you return to balance:

Sit in a comfortable chair with your feet flat on the floor.

Inhale through your nostrils with a steady breath for 5 counts.

Hold your breath for 5 counts.

Exhale for 10 counts.

Repeat.

With eyes open, look straight ahead.

Quickly, look up to the left for 2 counts and back to straight ahead.

Quickly, look down to the right for 2 counts and back to straight ahead.

Count out loud, slowly, 1...2...3...4...5

Hum the first bar of "Mary had a little lamb," or the "Birthday" song, or, an audible "Om" or "Hu."

Repeat counting and then humming.

Inhale through your nostrils with a steady breath for 5 counts.

Hold your breath for 5 counts.

Exhale for 10 counts.

With emotions now defused and the capacity to think with a calm mind, identify within your journal the problems that was derailing you (i.e. money, marriage, health, losses, etc.) and construct a problem-solving strategy to address each problem.

FICKLE MIND - CARNAL MIND

And we know that all things work together for good to those who love God, to those who are called according to His purpose. (Romans 8:28, NKJV)

The Apostle Paul wrote a very powerful and insightful epistle to the Church of Romans, where he explicitly distinguishes and separates the spiritually minded people from the carnal-minded people. When I thought about the above popular passage from the book of Romans, it alone, conveys a lot. I pondered on the first three words, "And we know…" I had to think about, who is the "we." Is it a "royal we" that indicates representatives of some others that really are the ones that know? Is it an "all-inclusive we" that suggests that everyone knows? Or, is it an "exclusive we" that suggest some know and others do not know? Apostle Paul draws a distinct demarcation between spiritually minded and carnal-minded people and further reduces this down to Christ-minded people that know; thus, I have included myself in this knowing. However, in parsing this out even further, I realize that I intellectually know that *all things work together for good to those who love God, to those who are called according to His purpose* and then it is revealed in my actions that I really don't know the above to be true.

Allow me to explain my fickle commitment to the truth of Paul's words. Periodically, I have purchased a two-dollar Powerball or Mega Millions lottery ticket. When the potential prize is generating national buzz hovering around half a billion dollars, I too, feel the allure of risking the loss of a few bucks on a likely losing lottery ticket for the quickly dashed hopes of winning an incredible amount of money once the numbers are read. "What is it," I ask, "that has me lusting for this monumental payday?" It must be something more than standing in front of the cameras to receive the oversized lottery check. After all, some others (including myself) would likely wish for a bit of anonymity; rather than receiving the 15 minutes of fame that a winner receives (followed by the constant pursuit of people with their hands out).

One is not likely to cash out a half-billion dollars and stow the money underneath a mattress, or stockpile a hefty amount of gold bullion that we'll admire while visiting a secure location. So, it is not the type of currency that gives the half-billion dollars its appeal; then it must be something else. Is it status? Power? Perceived respect? Is it convenience, comfort, or the ability to be the first in line? Is it an opportunity to amass, collect, or hoard material objects, hoping that others don't possess similar objects? Is it about adventure, entertainment, or association with the social or political elite? Is it about improving our health, augmenting our looks, or magnanimously gifting to the charitable needs of others?

Whatever I might wish for from my two dollar purchase and half-billion dollar winnings seems to put me in the camp of not truly knowing that *"…all things work for good for those who love God…"* It is only a two-dollar purchase but if feeds carnal notions by not relying on God to orchestrate the good that is to come into our lives. God is not trying to give us "stuff." God is hoping that what He has to give will resonate in the heart of humans more than the pursuit of "stuff." Though I am not typically enamored by "stuff" I find myself purchasing a half-billion dollar lottery ticket with its sole purpose to provide people with a lot of "stuff." Even when I allow myself to entertain the thought that the money is about safety and security, I am still disavowing God in favor of material pursuits. No amount of money will keep me well if I get sick. Of course, greater income gives one greater access to greater healthcare but we know that the "filthy rich" also get sick, writhing in discomfort as they ultimately await God's tender mercy to heal them. Consider the wonderful achievement of medical science to come up with the current vaccines in what has been dubbed "warp speed," we are still talking about introducing the non-contagious inoculant into the body to trick the body into preparing immunity fighting antibodies to fend off the onslaught of this virus.

At present, the odds of winning the Powerball lottery is 1 in 292.2 million and the Mega Millions is at 1 and 302 million. Of course, someone is going to win the jackpot but how many losing lottery tickets are being purchased to pay out a half of billion dollars when someone chooses the winning numbers? It is a sophisticated pyramid scheme that the state endorses to generate resources in a seemingly benign way. At two dollars a ticket, is there really any harm? Well, there is seemingly no harm for someone, like me, who can afford a random play at the lottery but for some, their addiction is fueled with the hopes of a big payday who can ill-afford the tickets. Furthermore, the egregious harm this insidious little purchase does is to divert our attention from God. It is a twisted ploy that places our salvation in the success of winning the lottery versus relying on God.

The Apostle Paul tells us in Galatians, "*So I say, walk by the Spirit, and you shall not gratify the desires of flesh. For the flesh desires what is contrary to Spirit, and the Spirit what is contrary to flesh. They are in conflict with each other, so you are not to do whatever you want.*" (5:16-17, NIV) I am mindful now that there are a lot of things I give myself over to the flesh. It is a constant tug because we do live in the world and are here upon the earth to have worldly experiences. Indeed, I've recently shared with a client who was beating himself up over all the poor choices he has made throughout his life and dubbing himself a "failure," that there was nothing he did that made him a failure. There is nothing that we have failed at; indeed, we can't fail, exhibiting competency at every developmental level.

I acknowledge that we spiritual beings having a human experience will be fraught with poor choices, faulty executions, faux pas, and heinous actions that are indicative of our "failure" to succeed (or progress) upon our spiritual journey, but it is not indicative of us being "failures" given that we are upon this earth to have a plethora of human experiences. To be human is not a success-only endeavor. The very nature of being human makes us fallible. The fallibility of our human experience shifts as we progress (or regress) on the spiritual continuum. Wherever we reside on the continuum for spiritual differentiation is exactly how we are to function developmentally. That is, a 16-year-old is not deemed a "failure" because he or she is not legally permitted to vote. And, nor is the 18-year-old who chooses not to vote a "failure." We can argue whether the 18-year-old is failing in his/her civic duty, but having a right and choosing not to implement it doesn't make the totality of the individual a "failure."

Not unlike my random purchase of lottery tickets that convey a fickle mind of claiming to trust in God, while trusting in the potential of winning millions of dollars, I see similarly conflicted souls in therapy. They come for healing; yet, intractably remain wedded to archaic ideas, self-defeating core beliefs and unhealthy interpersonal relationships. They languish in toxic work environments with little initiative to apply for a different job. They fight for their right to continual drug or alcohol usage; yet, vent their dissatisfaction about how their lives have turned out. They are failing in their chosen behaviors and remain stuck because they view themselves as failures. A client who laments that he is a failure due to his "right" to father a child but abdicating his "responsibility" to parent the child has certainly failed in his parenting obligations but he is not a failure. He simply performed at the degree of his emotional, psychological and spiritual developmental level. This is important because everyone exhibits behaviors at the level of their developmental competency. When we understand this we can quit trying to argue or debate with people at varying levels of spiritual differentiation.

Likewise, those entering therapy, which are brokenhearted and grieving the loss of their relationships that they failed to nurture, are not "failures." Selecting a partner to be in an intimate relationship with us is not by happenstance; it is purposeful. Indeed, the word "selecting" implies we are the one that is choosing another but there is a mutuality of decision between the two, based upon a narrow ten-point range of differentiation with intersections orchestrated by God. It may appear to be serendipities to the nonbeliever who reside on the opposite end of the country or on separate continents, meet in the same city, at the same airport, at the same time, awaiting connections for their ongoing flights, strike up a conversation as strangers but in short order the two are married. What is that? It is a divine spiritual connection and purposefully planned to facilitate each person's spiritual growth and development.

Each interconnection, whether a brief encounter by someone who nods, "hello," or from the person that snarls at us because he or she is having a bad day is purposeful and meaningful. More substantial interconnections with neighbors, colleagues, or friends are also purposeful and meaningful. Intimate connections with family members, confidantes, or lovers are purposeful and meaningful. Each momentary interaction shapes us for the next moment and the series of moments is the collective narrative of whom we are that determines our spiritual progression. That is, being acknowledged by a stranger (and our acknowledging of the stranger) lifts each of us up and out of self-focused egocentrism to an expansive, other-focused view. Not internalizing the snarls from a less evolved spiritual being become a testament to our spiritual maturity. When we are other-focused in a purposeful and meaningful way, it is hard to be self-indulgent (neurotic) with notions of failure.

The seemingly unsuccessful experiences that we have that are labeled "failures" are merely opportunities and lessons of life. The process of learning requires attentive focus and repetition. When we know that all things work together for good suggests that we have an attentive focus on God and experience God's Goodness despite the circumstances. We can weather losses, trials, and betrayals because there are lessons in the experience of living as humans and opportunities for us to grow spiritually. There is no fruit of the spirit associated with money, gold, or lottery tickets. The fruit of the spirit are concepts used to enhance our relationship with God, interaction among others, and within ourselves. The trek to spiritual wholeness aligns well with therapy; which is a process of healing. A fickle mind diverts us from the pathway of love, peace, joy, patience, faithfulness, goodness, kindness, gentleness, and self-control.

"And we know" is a "discerning mind" versus a "fickle mind;" thus, I have now purchased my last lottery ticket. However, I know this is a symbolic gesture and I'll have to keep marching forward on my spiritual trek, renouncing any allegiance to the material world. I have work to do and will endeavor to do it (with full knowledge of my fallible human nature). I also know that our psyche and soul are aligned, thus, psychology and spirituality are aligned. Psychology inclines toward self-actualization, integration, and wholeness. Spirituality inclines toward enlightenment, reintegration, and transcendence. Therapy requires problem identification, self-reflection or ownership of our role in creating/sustaining the problem and the desire to change ourselves or how we choose to relate to the problem. Spiritual healing requires awareness, confession of sin, and the renewal of one's mind. Psychopathology creates impairment in one's capacity to engage in leisure or peaceful quiescence within oneself, stable employment, and interpersonal relationships. Spiritual pathology impacts meaning/purpose (why we are here and what are we here to do), direction (where we are heading: hedonistic or Godly pursuits) and connection of who do we surround ourselves with (carnal-minded or spiritually minded).

The connections we have are powerful and Christ emphasized the church (as well as commanding that we loved God with all our mind, hearts, and soul; thereby, extending this love to others). As a therapist, I recognize the importance of human relationships on our mental health. Most mental health-seeking clients dread being alone and a main (not the only) causal factor of poor mental health is the feeling of insignificance and/or struggling close relationships. Some are fickle-minded in their relationships, not sure if they should go or stay. Others are committed to staying in a devitalized relationship, creating years of apathy and dysphoria. And, still others are engaged within toxic, conflict-habituated relationships. The purpose of all relationships is for the growth and development of the persons involved in the relationship.

Close, intimate relationships have the capacity to mimic the spiritual essence of God in physical form. We have the opportunity to learn, practice, and replicate each one of the fruit of the spirit. We learn patience and self-control as we endeavor to merge two lives together. We learn to develop and maintain civility in our kindness and gentleness with our tone. We elevate ourselves to a standard of conduct with goodness and exercise fidelity with our faithfulness. An intimate relationship develops peace *"which surpasses all understanding"* and joy (*"…My joy may remain in you and that your joy may be full.*" John 15:11, NKJV). Ultimately, we forge close, intimate relationships to experience the essence of love. Love happens in the pure heart realm even when we can't stand our lover/ partner. Love shows up when our children disappoint us. Love manifests despite disgruntled neighbors or cranky coworkers. Love is the universal currency used in our human transactions with one another.

I've discussed the concept of epistemology (how we know what we know) in my previous writings, but suffice to say that the "we that know" are those who "love God" (has awareness and a relationship with God), are told that "all things work together for good", but can that really be true? How do you tell the mother whose baby just died, the homeowner whose home burned to the ground, or the employee barely making it on the wages he was receiving that has just lost his job that "all things work together for good?" I am not telling the grieving mother, the dislocated homeowner, or the terminated employee don't worry because what you've experienced is good. Thus, we have to figure out what this "good" is and how does it apply to "those who know and love God?"

In our modern language, we love superlatives of "awesome, excellent, fantastic" over the seemingly mundane expression "good job." If I was to evaluate an employee as "good" or gave feedback on an academic paper as "good" it would likely crush the person's soul and move them to tears, but the dictionary tells us that "good" is above or superior to average. Do you remember what Christ said when He was called "good man?" Jesus said, *"Why do you call me good? No one is good but One, that is, God"* (Mark 10:17, NKJV). If we adhere to the basic trilogy in the language (i.e., "Father, Son, Holy Spirit," "red, yellow, green traffic lights," "good, bad & ugly," etc.), we can then see the superior nature of "good" (i.e., "poor = below standard; fair = standard & good = above standard).

So, God is Good...God is Above the Standard, or is the Standard that we all aspire to achieve, but I still haven't clarified how "all things work together for good?" Indulge me a bit more as I flesh out this concept of "good" just a bit more. "God is Good" therefore, God is Merciful and Just and with the losses I've referenced above, there doesn't appear to be anything "merciful or just" about them. Of course, this is contingent upon our narrow perspective. A child might rail, "I hate you, Mommy!" for not allowing her to eat cookies for breakfast or wear her favorite dress to play in the mud. Each of us makes meaning out of our distorted and limited perceptions in an attempt to understand the incomprehensible essence of God. In doing so, we start off with a logical fallacy.

In a world of impermanency and constant flux, time has relevancy and urgency for each of us experiencing this time-limited experience of our existence. Given everything stemming from the first breath we take is a gift to accommodate our physical experiences upon this earth that was never designed for permanent possession or hoarding, then it is not the substance of the child, home, or job that has any real relevancy to God. That is, God is beyond time and beyond these momentary experiences that we are having. The relevancy of the gift for us is to make meaning out of each and every one of these fleeting experiences. Whether something is good or bad is contingent upon how our minds make meaning of the experience. Somethings that are erroneously perceived as glorious (i.e., methamphetamines, heroin, etc.) can have a deleterious effect upon us; while adversities in the world can become a sharpening stone for our character.

Treating it all as good means that we are coming to truly know God, trust God, and appreciate God. The reason we equate God as Good is because we know that all things come from God and all things are good. God created the universe out of the void, order out of disorder, life from a lifeless planet and He called it all, "Good." Our misery comes to us not necessarily due to our circumstances or brevity upon this earth but with how our minds are making meaning out of these circumstances. The greater our alignment is with God, the greater our peace, joy, and recognition of goodness flowing from all things. *"And we know that all things work together for good to those who love God, to those who are called according to His purpose."* Christ has declared for us the trifold commandment aligned with our purpose. To love God with all of our hearts, minds, and souls and to love one another (as we are to love ourselves) is the ultimate purpose of which we are called. Let us practice the essence of love by disrupting our fickle minds that leads us to distress, discord, and dysfunction in a carnally based world by adopting spiritual mindfulness and replicating our love for God within our intimate relationships.

FEEDING THE SPIRIT

Oftentimes, when a relationship has become devitalized, we have lost a positive vision of God, our relationship (in general, and of our partner (specifically). If we focus upon bitterness, derisiveness, and discord that becomes the byproduct of the devitalized relationship. Take a renewed look at your relationship using the sentence stems below of positive attributes. Reflect upon them, write them out, and share them orally with your partner. While in session, a joining exercise I employ is to have Partner B sit adjacent to Partner A, with eyes closed. Following a few relaxing breaths, prepare to answer the sentence stems that Partner A reads. Partner A will gently, yet firmly, grasps partner B's left hand and slowly massage the hand (i.e. each finger, palm and top of hand) throughout the process as Partner B (with eyes closed) responds to the sentence stem that Partner A reads. When arriving at the last sentence stem, open your eyes and look directly into your partner's eyes and express "I love..." Reverse the process.

Dear _____,

I am grateful for...

I get excited about...

I feel cheerful...

It makes me smile when...

I recall how thoughtful...

It is important to...

I am choosing to create...

I am proud that...

I am hopeful for...

I appreciate...

I understand...

I see your point about...

I apologize...

I thank you for...

[Open your eyes, take both hands of your partner, look deeply in your partner's eyes and cite:]

I love...

DEVELOPING
SPIRITUAL MUSCLES

For where envy and self-seeking exist, confusion and every evil
thing are there. But the wisdom that is from above is first pure,
then peaceable, gentle, willing to yield, full of mercy and good
fruits, without partiality and without hypocrisy. Now the fruit of
righteousness is sown in peace by those who make peace.
(James 3:16-18, NKJV)

Have you heard people declare, "I'm spiritual…not religious?" They want
it known that they do have a spiritual essence and orientation but don't
want to associate themselves with a particular religion. They winch from
the embarrassment of "pedophile priests" and Protestant leaders engaging
in debauchery. They are dismayed by fellow pious, Sunday morning
parishioners gossiping about others on Monday or those engaging within
wanton behaviors on Friday night, seeking absolution two days later. They
struggle with the provincial views of the Bible challenging the credulity of
a liberal-minded, 21st Century generation. They avoid being branded by a
"religious" label by quickly referencing themselves as "spiritual." I certainly
understand this avoidance of a religious label as the Apostle Paul alluded
that one's renewed spiritual mind is not about labeling, *"…there is neither*
Greek nor Jew, circumcised nor uncircumcised, barbarian, Scythian, slave nor
free, but Christ is all and in all" (Colossians 3:11, NKJV).

It may sound like a blasphemous statement but there are really no Christians
in heaven. There are no Buddhists, Muslims, Hindus or Jews in heaven
because there is no religion in heaven. Religion is a social construction

that is both useful and dysfunctional. Religion is useful as a tool to help construct and develop our spirituality. When religion is dysfunctional (i.e., ceasing to function) it oppresses, distorts, and diverts our spiritual progression. Throughout history, people have used religious bigotry to whack others over the head with their hypocritical piety. However, there is some value in people coming together in a like-minded fashion to edify spiritual understanding, hone spiritual muscles to advance further along the spiritual pathway.

The pathway to the pure-heart realm begins in the indifferent-heart realm ("*For where envy and self-seeking exist, confusion and every evil thing are there*"). Our ignorance is profound and even our adherence to religious ideas in the indifferent-heart realm is perverse. Consider Neo-Nazi sympathizers or those affiliated with the Ku Klux Klan who espouses a love of God and a disdain for others. Hate groups of all stripes justify separation from others with notions of superiority. It is curious (and tragic) to see people espouse superior notions of race, gender, religiosity, etc. with specious evidence to justify their superiority. They attribute their self-seeking interests as being endorsed by God but God doesn't abide in the indifferent-heart realm.

Our vision of spirituality in the indifferent-heart realm is opaque, with fundamental and perfunctory religious expressions. I've yet to find a therapeutic intervention or a logical argument that bumps people residing in the indifferent-heart realm into the craving-heart realm. In the year 2020, I was more convinced of this than ever, having seen so many people endorse the losing presidential candidate, Trump. It was interesting to see that people were willing to dismantle democracy in favor of an authoritarian despot. Of course, if I was a better historian I shouldn't be surprised at how these political strongmen capture the appeal of people and having them behave counter to the principles and values they have purported to have. We have had the term "alternative facts" added to our lexicon as a cover for a president that lies with impunity and a huge swath of the American population enabling his lies. Isaiah warns, "*Woe to those who call evil good, and good evil; Who put darkness for light, and light for darkness; Who put bitter for sweet, and sweet for bitter!*" (Isaiah, 5:20, NKJV).

Given that I am not a historian, theologian, or statistician, I can't tell you if my following supposition is true. What I do know is that human life is fragile and our time here is limited. The Garden of Eden appeared to have been a cooperative venture between God, nature, and "man" (woman). Adam and Eve had no strife in the Garden. There was no pestilence, strife, or fear of animals. I don't believe that either Adam or Eve could have ever imagined the impact of our adversarial relationship with nature once their actions caused them to be expelled from the Garden. Nature has wreaked havoc upon humans. Not only has our lifespan been considerably shortened since the days of Adam (i.e. Methuselah living ten times longer than those during our current lifespan), fragile human beings have been decimated with hurricanes, tornados, floods, famine, contagions, diseases, plagues, epidemics, pandemics, etc.

We are in a constant battle to subdue, tame, or have dominion over nature. Nature cooperates at times but then it contests us. When Mother Nature has indigestion the ground shakes, volcanoes erupt, and buildings topple. With a fickle mood, Mother Nature can miserly withhold rain from desperately needed crops and then, seemingly out of spite, unleash a torrent of rain that strips farmers of any sliver of hope that salvaging their crops is possible. Nature doesn't care about affluence or poverty. Try building your mansion in a pristine, exclusive, forested area and watch the insatiable appetite of a wildfire consume your home as a famished party guest consumes your hors d'oeuvres. And, lest you think nature has compassion for the poor, watch that hope being dashed from a famine-starved community when loci fly in to devour what crops remain.

Nature is necessary for human survival upon this planet but nature also kills. Herein lies my supposition: I believe that we humans have tortured, maimed, killed, and devastated the lives of one another far more than nature. I don't have facts to back this supposition up but there can be undeniable cruelty lurking in the hearts of humans. How many wars have we've engaged in, perhaps family members on the other side, with thousand, upon thousands, upon thousands killed? How many innocent people have been caught up in collateral damage from waring combatants? What is the impact on those family members who lose a mother or father, sister or brother, aunt or uncle to the atrocities of war? What is the societal impact of those who return as amputees, or with TBI's or PTSD? What is the financial cost of war that infringe upon efforts to obtain universal health care, infrastructure development, or freeing students from the strangling grip of student loan debt?

When we see people as the "other" then we can exploit them, take advantage of them, disregard them and even kill them. When we forge camps, even religious camps, we reinforce the "other" dynamic that allows us to have disregard of others. James stated above *"For where envy and self-seeking exist, confusion and every evil thing are there."* I am not advocating that we throw religion away; to the contrary, as I like religion. What I am advocating for is that we grow beyond our religion. Use the religion as an entrée into spirituality and to develop spirituality, we must develop spiritual muscles. Religion can be like the apparatus we find in our local gym that we use for physical development, to enhance our spiritual development.

I have once heard that the distinction between religion and spirituality is that "religion tells you the truth and spirituality allows you to discover truth." This is not a bad definition in that those institutions or individuals that purport to know the "truth" have a tendency to "impose that truth" upon others, but it is still a vague definition. I've made an attempt at defining and operationalizing spirit in my previous works but suffice to say, the spiritual essence of ourselves consists of ascertaining the meaning for our existence, determining purpose that is contingent upon the meaning of our existence, recognition or awareness of the direction we are heading in life and selectively choosing our connections. Within the superior hierarchy of spirit at the helm, mind charting the course and the body getting us there, we grant greater credence to the reverse order of body, mind, and spirit.

Though we tend to grant primacy to the physical body in this material world, the body has no agency or permanency on its own. The mind grants the body agency but it, too, lacks permanency on its own. An enduring spirit has permanency and certainly, all human beings have an animated spirit to give life to this "lump of clay" that represents our physical being and to grant us agency. Spirit is the executor of mind and body and not unlike what Jesus said during His crucifixion, "Forgive them, Father, as they know not what they do" I will add that many of us, "know not who we are." To develop spiritual muscles, we must first be aware of whom we are as spiritual beings and then Zukav takes us a bit further. Gary Zukav asserts in his book, The Mind of the Soul, "You can visualize, meditate, and pray, but until you are willing to assume responsibility for what you create, you cannot grow spiritually because spirituality and responsibility are inseparable."

I concur with Zukav's assertion that the development of spirituality and responsibility are inseparable because in the pure-heart, spiritual realm one has to have the knowledge of who we are and what we are here to do; along with engaging within appropriate action. Knowledge plus action is responsibility. It is akin to what Maya Angelou says, "When you know better, do better." And the Apostle Paul said to the Corinthians, *"But the natural man does not receive the things of the Spirit of God, for they are foolish to him; nor can he know them because they are spiritually discerned. But he who spiritually judges all things, yet he himself is rightly judged by no one."* (Corinthians 2:14-15, NKJV)

Developing spiritual muscles is not complex. Nothing related to spirituality is complex; although, the spiritual economy can be counterintuitive (i.e. "it is better to give than receive" or "love your enemies"). Not unlike redefining our physical physique in the material world that may require us going to the gym and pushing against the resistance of a weighted bar, when we are developing spiritual muscles we push against resistance. The material world has tremendous gravitational forces, pulling us toward self-indulgence, avarice, and hedonism; therefore, in developing spiritual muscles is saying, "No," or pushing against the resistance of this gravitational force. Every disciple met with an ignominious death because the world of darkness hated the light of Christ that these disciples carried. At one point, Peter ran away when he was being accused of knowing Christ. When developing his spiritual muscles within his conviction in Christ Jesus, Peter pushed back on the world, even to the point of his death (being crucified upside down). *"If the world hates you, you know that the world hated Me before it hated you"* (John 15:18, NKJV).

Missouri is the "show me" state but I dare say that this is the attitude of virtually all people in the Western world. Westerners value empiricism and scientific methods to understand the material world. This makes sense as one must use the most appropriate measuring device to acquire data for the object one is interested in knowing about. That is, we don't use a tape measurer to determine the volume of a liquid and we don't use a measuring cup to measure the width of a room. Additionally, how do we measure the circumference of a line or the angles of a circle? Empiricism touts that all knowledge stems from sensory experiences and scientific methods is the way we go about collecting that data and drawing some conclusions about that data. "Show me God," the skeptic may decry, "in a way that I can perceive Him with my sensory measures."

As of this writing, there are currently two vaccines vying for emergency approval from the FDA that boast of a 90-95 percent efficacy rate of halting infection from this world's pandemic. If that holds true, and the side effects are minimal, what a scientific boon for combating the horrific Coronavirus. Science can be proud and society can be grateful. Of course, there remains people holding onto the attitude of "show me" to see this efficacy plays itself out in the general population before they consider taking the vaccine but this scientific achievement is akin to the space race and landing men on the moon. The efficacy of these vaccines will not be measured with hope or prayers, but with empirical measures to determine the percentage of those vaccinated who are protected from contracting the virus. This makes sense, as natural means are gauged effective (or not) with natural measures.

However, one cannot measure an imperceptible spirit with any device used to observe or measure phenomena in the material world. In developing our spiritual muscles (or simply cultivating bountiful fruit), we look to see what we want to augment in the spiritual world. I've referenced the fruit of the spirit throughout this book and each one of them needs to be developed to enhance our spirituality. Faith is the antithesis of empiricism because we can't taste, touch, smell, see, or hear faith. *"Now faith is the substance of the things hoped for, the evidence of things not seen."* (Hebrews 11:1, NKJV). We are told that everyone has a measure (modicum) of faith; which, implies that faith can be developed. When we trust in God by pushing back on our doubts and fears, we increase our faith.

FEEDING THE SPIRIT

It is hard to develop spiritual quiescence or spiritual calm when we are living a hurried existence and have a disturbed mind. The action of "doing" feeds the world. The state of "being" feeds the soul. The following ten coping strategies can allow you to decompress from a frazzled day; thus, regenerating your calm. When we are spiritually calm we have a greater ability to tap into the Essence of God to generate greater clarity for decision making and human connections.

1) Deep Breathing

Spirit is considered a "life-giving force" and the Bible informs us that God animated this spiritual life force by breathing into the nostrils of man. Modern CPR techniques no longer use mouth-to-mouth respiration to bring this life force back into the person who has lost the capacity to breathe, but during these COVID-19 days a respirator is a prime piece of medical equipment that helps to keep those afflicted with the virus alive. Thus, breath is important for life and important for spiritual calm. At the top of each hour, breathe in deeply through your nose for 5 counts. Hold it for 5 counts and expel the air through your mouth for 10 counts. Repeat the process but the entire process should not take more than a minute. With your in-breath breathe in peace or any calming spiritual concept; while expelling with your out-breath any discursive thoughts/feelings you may have.

2) Prayer

Prayer is the conduit that accesses the Ultimate. It taps us into the expansiveness of the Most High God and replenishes our soul. Prayer can happen any time and at its core, it is simply talking with God. We can talk with God doing the dishes, driving the car, mowing the lawn, or between therapy sessions for us clinicians needing to reset ourselves between therapy clients, and for clients trying to regulate their volatile emotional affect. From a psychological perspective, I have equated prayer as a form of cognitive restructuring in changing maladaptive thoughts.

3) Meditation

Meditation need not be so esoteric, foreign, or mystical. You don't have to contemplate your navel or prostrate yourself into various yoga positions to strive for Nirvana. Just like the simplicity of prayer that has us talking with God, meditation can be a deliberate mental focus to listening to God. With mindfulness of breath, focus on a singular spiritual concept (e.g. love) and listen for God's whispered wisdom.

4) Art

Tapping into the imperceptible or even raw emotion may defy word choices. Art is a way to access emotion, thoughts, or spirit when words are not enough. Art access that creative part of ourselves and this can come out in many ways. Painting, drawing, photography, adult coloring books, interior designing or just rearranging the room is an artistic endeavor. Tinkering with a car or baking can also be considered artistic endeavors that symbolize our creative capacity.

5) Animals

Dogs are said to be "man's best friend," but the reality is that any creature that you have an affinity for (e.g. rabbits, snakes, fish, rats, bugs, birds, cats, etc.) can alleviate stress, take you out of an angry/depressive mood and tap into transcendent love of God's creation. Spirituality shifts our focus from the limiting view of ourselves while expanding love to another life form.

6) Social Support Network

The Bible informs us that God told Adam that it is not good for man to be alone; thus, he created Eve, but we also need family, friends, the community, and others to connect with. Christ talked about the importance of the Church and this is where like-minded individuals come together for edification and support. Joining AA, NA, senior citizen or social media groups makes connections to pull people out of their doldrums and mimic spiritual connections.

7) Music

There are gifted gospel singers and choirs that can stoke our emotions and cause tears to stream down our faces, with chills running down our spines, but so can other genres of music. Music can have universal appeal. Music can get us out of our heads, into our emotions and facilitate spiritual transcendence.

8) Positive Self-Talk

God spoke into being the creation of the heavens and earth. We often speak into being the creation of our experiences through thought and emotions. "I AM" is the name God used when sending Moses back to Egypt and is the affirmation we can use to change our cognitions. "I am… worthy…thoughtful…kind…etc. is just a few affirming words that align our heads and hearts with spirit.

9) Writing/Journaling

Aaah…I enjoy writing, and you might find this enjoyable too. Writing is a therapeutic tool but can also aid in our connection with the Ultimate. Writing is an externalizing process to become self-reflective, analyze themes or patterns, purging discursive emotions, and facilitating our study/understanding of God.

10) Physical Activity and Dance

Whirling Dervish dancers spin with their right hand toward heaven and the left hand toward the earth and enter into a trance-like state depicting the interconnection of God and humanity. The Bible states *"Let them praise His name with the dance…"* (Psalms 149:3, NKJV). Dance (and physical activity) increases the endorphins in our brain; thus, enhancing our mood. Our enhanced mood generates spiritual quiescence.

EPILOGUE

The pathway to peace, integration of self, and reunification with an All-Encompassing God is an arduous one within our physical existence because it is often contingent upon cogent self-effort, servitude to often ungrateful others, and choosing the intangible gifts of God over material acquisitions. This pathway is unattainable while we remain ignorant in the indifferent-heart realm, because the hedonistic pursuits of this realm are purely self-indulgent. Self-indulgence is the antithesis of God and those who operate out of this realm, even those who attest to the existence of God, have no knowledge or relationship with God. This pathway is short-lived in the craving-heart realm. It is here that we have glimpses of the pure-heart realm but tainted with the incessant desires of ego to compare, compete, contrast, and to one-up our aspirations over another. The pathway to peace in the pure-heart realm is simple, as all such things in the spiritual (pure-heart) realm is simple. There is no need for philosophical undertakings or scientific inquiries; it requires our devotion and commitment to the Architect of Peace.

With our minds centered upon God, those residing within the pure-heart realm live simple lives. Those who reside in the pure-heart realm are service-oriented, humble, serene, and faith-based. The Apostle Paul instructs us, *"Let nothing be done through selfish ambition or conceit, but in lowliness of mind let each esteem others better than himself. Let each of you look out not only for his own interests, but also for the interests of others"* (Philippians 2: 3-4, NKJV). In my spiritual maturation from the indifferent-heart realm to the pure-heart realm my mind became clearer, my heart is more open and my efforts to serve are realized in my private, public, and professional life. The more I evolved spiritually, the more I was drawn to volunteer services. Ultimately, this penchant to serve led me to a master's degree in social work and a doctorate degree in psychology. I've often said that one gets a degree in social work to serve others and one gets a degree in psychology to figure oneself out. I hate using pejoratives, especially in the field of psychology when people are easily stigmatized but those of us pursuing study in the field of psychology are undoubtedly a little "nuts." We are wounded warriors coming to the aid of others when we really just need to fix ourselves. Some of the disorders we are scanning for in our clients to affix a diagnostic label, many of us (therapists) are struggling with ourselves. Yes, I am still trying to figure myself out and I suspect the journey to self-discovery is never-ending.

God is not looking for a perfect me. God is not looking for a perfect you. God is looking for someone like David, "a man after his own heart" (Acts 13:22). In ending how I began with Bishop T.D. Jakes' powerful and poetic words, "feed that which feeds you," attentive focus, worship, prayer, praise, etc. feeds into God. In doing so, we access God by choosing Him who has already chosen us by creation. We are nourished by the spiritual fruit that the Apostle Paul lays out for us in Galatians. Feeding the spirit heals a fragmented psyche to bolster our mental health. Per Apostle Paul, *"Be anxious for nothing, but to everything by prayer and supplication, with thanksgiving, let your requests be made known to god, and the peace of God, which surpasses all understanding, will guard your hearts and minds through Christ Jesus"* (Philippians 4:6-7, NKJV).

GLOSSARY

Abraham	(1948-1638 BC) Patriarch of the three major monotheistic religions of Judaism, Christianity, and Islam.
Adam	(3760-2830 BC) God's first human creation, partnered with Eve; thus, purported to be the progenitor of the human race.
Agnostic	Skeptic regarding the existence of God. It is not a definitive view that God does not exist but the existence of God is unknowable.
Atheist	The assertion that no God exists or has ever existed.
Christ/Christian	Christos (anointed one) a title attributed to the Messiah or Jesus of Nazareth establishing a following of adherents-Christianity, representing a fundamental split from Judaism in the 1st Century. Jesus is a part of the spiritual triune (Father, Son, Holy Spirit).
COVID-19	Coronavirus Disease pandemic originating in Wuhan China in 2019. A severe, acute respiratory virus wreaking havoc in the human population worldwide.
Craving-heart	Second realm on the spiritual differentiation scale signifying rationalism, intellectualizing, egocentrism, hierarchy separations; along with competition and comparisons.

Deism	Belief in a non-involved Supreme Entity that sets creation in motion with a hands-off stance.
DSM-5	Diagnostic Statistical Manual (of Mental Disorders) 5th Edition. Clusters symptoms to diagnoses and differentiate mental disorders.
Ego-centrism	Placing the individual self at the center of the universe with an emphasis on "me vs. we."
Gandhi, M., K.	(1869-1948) Mohandas Karamchand Gandhi (Mahatma = "Great One") was an Indian born, Hindu lawyer, activist promoting ahimsa (non-violence) as a way of life and strategic tactic within demonstrations and protests against British rule.
Hedonism	A philosophy and psychology of self-interest, pleasure-seeking approach to life with the goal of increasing pleasure and reducing pain.
Humanist	A philosophy that is human-centric in endorsing/promoting human values, agency, rights, development, intellect, scholarship, culture, arts, etc. with downplay of God.
Jakes, T.D.	(1957-) Thomas Dexter Jakes, Sr. Bishop of the nondenominational church, The Potter's House. Prolific writer, producer, filmmaker, and former talk show host.
Indifferent-heart Realm	The first of three developmental stages on the spiritual differentiation scale with spiritual ignorance, hedonism and self-indulgence.
Internal Family System (IFS)	An integrated psychotherapy approach developed by Richard Schwartz in the 1980s that uses system's view of the mind with infinite subparts.
Limbic System	A part of the brain that is comprised of structures that include the amygdala, hypothalamus, thalamus, etc., where emotion resides.

Malcolm X	(1925-1965) an American Muslim Minister of the Nation of Islam and civil rights advocate was born Malcolm Little, initially discounting slave name with an X, and assumed the name of El-Hajj Malik El-Shabazz.
Martin Luther King, Jr.	(1929-1968) An American Baptist Pastor and civil rights leader who embraced non-violence with civil disobedience.
Micro-aggressions	Subtle or indirect statements or actions that reinforce the marginalization of individuals within a particular "outsider" group that communicates hostility or disdain for the outsider (e.g., snubs, sarcasm, slights, etc.).
Monotheism	A belief in a singular God and the underpinning of the three major religions of Judaism, Christianity and Islam.
Moses	(1526-1406 BC). Israeli born child avoided the Pharaoh's death edict by being adopted into the Pharaoh's own household, became the emancipator, lawgiver, and author of the first five books of the Bible.
Maya Angelou	(1928-2014). American poet, essayist, author, and civil rights activist.
Noah	(2948-1998 BC). The Biblical character known for building a great ark to house all life that would survive the great, world-destroying flood.
Pagan	Those who deviate from or non-adherence to the world's major monotheistic religions (i.e. animism, Wicca, Buddhism, etc.).
Polytheism	A belief in multiple deities existing at the same time (i.e. Hinduism, Egyptian deities, Ancient Greek Gods, etc.)

167

Pure-heart Realm	Third realm on the spiritual differentiation scale signifying spiritual enlightenment, empathy, compassion; adherence to faith and exemplifying behaviors/actions that are congruent with spiritual ideals.
Religion	Is the method, structure, doctrine, congregates, and/or belief system design for the enhancement of spiritual development.
Spirit	The non-physical essence and apex of the triune self (spiritual, mental, physical) that is comprised of meaning, purpose, direction and connection.
Spiritual Differentiation	A means to operationalize and measure spiritual progression within three spiritual realms (indifferent-heart, craving-heart & pure-heart).
Theism	A belief in an overarching entity (God) that is not only the Creator but remains actively involve within His Creation.

REFERENCES

Adler, M. J., (1980). How to think about god: A guide for the 20th century pagan. USA

Barnes, C. & Wills, M. (2019). Overcoming the stigma of mental illness: Embracing our fears and increasing our empathy. https://www.psychologytoday.com/us/blog/mental-illness-america/201909/overcoming-the-stigma-mental-illness

Bourne, E. J., (2010, 5th Edition). The anxiety & phobia workbook. New Harbinger Publications. Oakland, CA

Brach, T., Radical compassion in challenging times. Psychotherapy Networker (May/June, 2020). North Hollywood, CA

Carter, J., (2018). Faith: A journey for all. Simon and Schuster. NY, NY.,

Carter, S. L. (1996). Integrity. Harper Collins. NY, NY.

Diagnostic and Statistical Manual of Mental Disorders, 5th Edition, (2013). American Psychiatric Association. Arlington, VA

Holloway, A. L. (2016). The ugli fruit: Tapping the inner spirit for greater mental health. iUniverse. Bloomington, IN

Garfinkel, R. (2017). American Anxiety: American's Voice Speaks in Anxious Tones. https://www.psychologytoday.com/us/blog/time-out/2017/american-anxiety

King, Jr., M. L. (2010 reprint). Strength to love. Fortress Press, Minneapolis, MN

Meacham, J. (2020). The hope of glory: Reflections on the last words of Jesus from the cross. Convergent Books. NY, NY.

National Alliance of Mental Illness: https://www.nami.org

Osborn, A.W. (1963). The axis and the rim: A modern quest for reality. A Quest Book. The Theosophical Publishing House, Wheaton, IL.

Schwartz, R. (September/October 2020). Working with our internalized racism: From shame to unburdening. Psychotherapy Networker. Psychotherapynetworker.org

Strong, J. (1996). The new Strong's exhaustive concordance of the bible. Thomas Nelson Publishers, Inc., Nashville, TN.

Vanzant, I., (2013). Forgiveness: 21 Days to forgive everyone for everything. Smiley Books. Carlsbad, CA

Zukav, G. & Francis, L. (2003). The mind of the soul: Responsible choice. Free Press (Simon and Schuster, Inc.). NY, NY.

ABOUT THE AUTHOR

Dr. Al L. Holloway is a psychologist and clinical social worker, currently residing in a rural, Southwestern, Minnesota community (Marshall, MN). He provides mental health services within a variety of treatment modalities with the recognition of spiritual preeminence of the triune self (i.e., spiritual, mental, and physical). He implements traditional therapeutic approaches purportedly designed for psychological healing; along with the inclusion of spiritual modalities (i.e., affirmations, meditation, prayer, etc.) to facilitate growth and development upon the spiritual continuum toward wholeness. Previous works include: The Ugli Fruit: Tapping into the Inner Spirit; The Fruit of the Spirit: A Primer for Spiritual Minded Social Workers; and Break the Chains, Free the Heart: A Spiritual Pathway through Healing, Transformation and Mental Health.

Printed in the United States
by Baker & Taylor Publisher Services